As the summer app... raise your tempera...

Don't miss the first book in all ...
ROYAL BRIDES, by favorite author Lucy Monroe.
The Prince's Virgin Wife is a tale of an irresistible alpha
prince, an innocent virgin and the passion that
ignites between them. In part two of Julia James's
glamorous MODELS & MILLIONAIRES duet—
For Pleasure...or Marriage?—enter a world of
sophistication and celebrity, populated by beautiful
women and a gorgeous Greek tycoon! *Captive in His Bed*
is part two of Sandra Marton's Knight Brothers trilogy.
This month we follow the passionate adventures of tough
guy Matthew. And watch out, this story is in our UNCUT
miniseries and that means it's *hot!*

We've got some gorgeous European men for you
this month. *The Italian's Price* by Diana Hamilton
sees an Italian businessman go after a woman who's
stolen from his family, but what will happen when
desire unexpectedly flares between them? In
The Spanish Billionaire's Mistress by Susan Stephens,
a darkly sexy Spaniard and a young Englishwoman
clash. He thinks she's just out for her own gain—yet
the physical attraction between them is too strong for
him to stay away. In *The Wealthy Man's Waitress* by
Maggie Cox, a billionaire businessman falls for a
young Englishwoman and whisks her off to Paris for
the weekend. He soon discovers that she is not just a
woman for a weekend....

Check out www.eHarlequin.com for a list of recent
Presents books! Enjoy!

Models
& Millionaire$

*Escape to a world of absolute
wealth, glamour and romance...*

Escape to a world of absolute wealth and
glamour in this brand-new duet from Julia James.
These models find themselves surrounded by
beauty and sophistication. It can be a false
world, but fortunately there are strong alpha
millionaires waiting in the wings to claim them!

Julia James

FOR PLEASURE...
OR MARRIAGE?

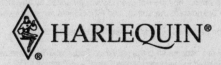

TORONTO • NEW YORK • LONDON
AMSTERDAM • PARIS • SYDNEY • HAMBURG
STOCKHOLM • ATHENS • TOKYO • MILAN • MADRID
PRAGUE • WARSAW • BUDAPEST • AUCKLAND

ISBN 0-373-12536-4

FOR PLEASURE...OR MARRIAGE?

First North American Publication 2006.

This edition published by arrangement with Harlequin Books S.A.

www.eHarlequin.com

Printed in U.S.A.

All about the author...
Julia James

JULIA JAMES lives in England with her family. Harlequin novels were the first "grown-up" books Julia read as a teenager, and she's been reading them ever since.

Julia adores the English countryside (and the Celtic countryside!), in all its seasons, and is fascinated by all things historical, from castles to cottages. She also has a special love for the Mediterranean. She considers both ideal settings for romance stories! Since becoming a romance writer, she has, she says, had the great good fortune to start discovering the Caribbean, as well, and is happy to report that those magical, beautiful islands are also ideal settings for romance stories! "One of the best things about writing romance is that it gives you a great excuse to take vacations in fabulous places!" says Julia. "And all in the name of research, of course!"

Her first stab at novel writing was Regency romances. "But alas, no one wanted to publish them!" she says. She put her writing aside until her family commitments were clear, and then renewed her love affair with contemporary romances to great success.

In between writing, Julia enjoys walking, gardening, needlework and baking "extremely gooey chocolate cakes"—and trying to stay fit!

CHAPTER ONE

MARKOS MAKARIOS STROLLED with a lithe, leisurely gait across the *parvis* in front of Nôtre Dame. Although it was crowded with tourists, all ogling the stupendous cathedral at the southern end of the wide area, he did not object to their presence. It was good, sometimes, to mingle with the masses. Not, he knew, that it made his security people feel comfortable when he did so. Both Taki and Stelios, discreetly following him, wouldn't relax entirely until he was safely back in his limo.

But the warm September day was far too fine for sitting inside a limo crawling through traffic, Paris obscured by smoked glass, with nothing to do but study the latest communiqués from his direct reports around Europe. The sudden restless impulse to abandon wheeled transport as the limo had gained the Ile de la Cité had been the right one. Besides, he would probably reach his destination on the Ile St Louis faster on foot.

Not—he suppressed a flicker of irritation—that he was in any particular hurry to reach his scheduled appointment. Lunch with the chairman of the French company he was currently in negotiations with would be a long-drawn-out and inevitably tedious affair.

A flicker of boredom nudged at him. It was becoming

familiar, and its arrival irritated him as much as the prospect of the lunch ahead. He had no reason to be bored. None at all. He was in the prime of life—a fit and healthy thirty-three—with a lifestyle that every man in the world would envy him for. The Makarios wealth saw to that!

With the single exception of the one element of his life that he could, frustratingly, do nothing about—the constant, exasperating importuning of his father for him to perpetuate the Makarios dynasty—he had everything he could possibly want. Riches, property in whichever part of the world took his fancy, a yacht in the Mediterranean and another in the Caribbean, a personal jet he flew himself when he was inclined, any number of top marque cars—and, of course, as many beautiful women as he wanted.

And yet—

Again, he felt that creeping sense of *ennui* flicker around him. He needed to dispel it.

By any means necessary. Including, as he was now doing, acting out of character. Taking a walk across one of the most popular tourist spots in Paris, just like any other tourist.

He paused and lifted his eyes to the magnificent west front of the most famous cathedral in Europe, with its twin towers of glittering Caen stone, the vast rose window nested below, and the great arched entrances. Around him, tourists were chattering in all languages, cameras flashing, groups posing, guidebooks lifted and perused.

'Oh, will you just leave me *alone?!*'

The vehement, infuriated voice just to his right drew his attention from the cathedral. As his eyes flicked sideways, he registered two things. The speaker had spoken in English, not French—and she was the most stunning female he'd seen in a long, long time.

It was the hair that registered first. A fantastic sunburst tumble of curls, cascading down her back almost to her waist, the colour of topaz caught with rich gold light. For a moment it dazzled him, taking all his attention. But then, with the perfectly honed instincts of the practised connoisseur of fine women, his gaze moved on to her face.

And stopped.

She could have stepped out of a pre-Raphaelite painting. An oval face, translucent skin, lustrous eyes and a rich, sensuous mouth. But her features were not arranged in the serenity of a painted image. Oh, no—Markos felt amusement tugging at his mouth—serene was the last word to describe her at this moment!

She was fizzing with exasperation, her expressive, long-lashed amber eyes snapping, jaw set tight.

And he could see exactly why. Two young men were blocking her way, grinning knowingly, glancing at each other, and then one of them was accosting her again in broken English, trying to get her to go and have a drink with them.

'No!' the redhead reiterated. 'Leave me alone!'

The other of the two young men put out his hand to her, taking her wrist. She made to shake it off angrily, but he only laughed and repeated his unwanted invitation.

Markos found himself stepping towards her. A few succinct, highly vernacular phrases in fluent French came from him. The two young men froze. Markos added one more sibilant instruction, and then smiled. It was a smile without humour.

The young man dropped the girl's wrist as if it had suddenly turned red hot, and without more ado he and his companion bolted off.

'*Merci, m'sieu.*'

The voice was stiff, the accent English.

'My pleasure,' returned Markos urbanely, in her own language. His accent, thanks to his English mother, was all but perfect, he knew. He also knew it didn't go with his appearance, which was not English at all.

He could see her expression registering the dissonance.

He could also see it registering something else entirely. Something that sent a spear of satisfaction shafting through him. For a moment he just let her gaze, then, timing it perfectly, he murmured, 'I fear, however, that they will not be the last to...importune you.'

The flash of amber came again, and the tightening of the beautiful rich mouth.

'Why can't they just leave me *alone?*' she demanded with rhetorical exasperation.

A laugh broke from him. Quite genuine. He spread his hands. 'Because this is Paris. It's what men do here. Pursue beautiful women.'

'It's just so annoying!' she exclaimed. 'And it's so *stupid,* too! What kind of man thinks he can just pick up a girl in the street, for heaven's sake?'

Not a flicker showed in Markos's eyes. 'What you need,' he said smoothly, 'is a bodyguard.'

Amber eyes rested on him. There was uncertainty in them now, not annoyance. And a lot more than uncertainty.

But the uncertainty won.

Her lips pressed together repressively. 'Good day, *m'sieu.* Thank you for what you did just now.' She started to move off.

Markos watched her go. She got about twenty metres before a lanky Scandinavian stopped her, guidebook in hand, asking her the way, then pointing invitingly towards the cathedral entrance. The girl shook her head, and the sunlight dazzled in her glorious hair. She moved sideways around the Scandinavian and straight into the path of a North African, who fell into step beside her, oblivious of her attempts to repulse him.

With no change in his leisurely gait, Markos strolled towards her. The creeping edge of *ennui* started to dissolve.

* * *

Fury fizzed through Vanessa again. This was just unbearable! Her very first day in Paris and she was being pestered to death. Whether she stood still or kept walking, they just kept coming. And all she wanted was to be left in peace to do what had been a dream for years and years—see the glories of the most beautiful city in Europe.

'*Va't'en!*' she snapped at the one trying to talk to her now. 'Get lost. Leave me alone!'

'Eenglish?' said the man, and grinned. 'I show you good time.'

Then, from just behind her, a new voice spoke. It wasn't a language she knew, but she recognised the voice. Her head whipped round.

It was that man again. The man who'd got rid of those two Frenchmen. Who'd said that this was Paris and what else should she expect but to be pestered. Words to that effect. Who'd told her she needed a bodyguard.

Who was the most devastating male she'd ever seen.

Her eyes swept over him again. Dear God, but he really was jaw-dropping. Not French, she thought. He was powerfully built, tall, but with a kind of casual continental elegance to him that was almost sensual in its effect. Yet he'd spoken English without an accent, despite his dark hair, his Mediterranean skin tone. She couldn't tell what nationality he was. He'd spoken English to her, French to those pests and something else—Arabic?—to this one.

Whatever nationality he was, he made the breath stop in her lungs.

But she mustn't let him. Mustn't do anything as stupid as respond to his incredible looks in any way! The last thing she needed was to give any male—even this one!—the slightest sign of encouragement.

Even though he *had* come to her rescue twice in a row.

The North African had vanished as if he'd never been. She took a short breath.

'Thank you,' she said to her rescuer, as stiffly as she could.

He seemed undeterred by her coolness. 'You know, you really do need a bodyguard,' he observed. 'These foreign johnnies are the very devil.'

His accent had changed suddenly, with his second sentence, from normal English to the old-fashioned speech of a pre-war film.

Vanessa glanced up at him—he really was very tall, and she was no muppet herself heightwise. Humour was sparking in his eyes.

They're grey. I thought they were black, but they're not. They're a very dark grey...

The irrelevant observation distracted her a moment. Then the expression in his eyes got her. For a second it hung in the balance.

Then she fell.

She felt her lips quirk. 'Are you trying to tell me you're not a "foreign Johnny"?'

'I'm probably more English than you are,' he replied urbanely.

'What?' Her face furrowed.

The dark grey eyes flickered over her. 'Only Celts have red hair,' he murmured.

'Scottish grandmother,' Vanessa acknowledged.

There was something wrong with her speaking voice. It was sounding breathy, and more high-pitched than usual. She swallowed. She mustn't stand here talking to a complete stranger, even if he had rescued her twice from unwanted admirers—

It was as if he was reading her mind.

'You know,' he went on, and his voice had that smooth note in it again, that did strange things to her insides, 'there is no need at all to be suspicious. I really am very respectable.

And, if you would allow me—' the note in his voice changed slightly '—I would be more than happy to walk with you around the cathedral—if that is what you were intending—and ensure you are not pestered.'

He smiled down at her, and Vanessa found herself searching his face. There was nothing in it except a bland politeness. For a moment she felt—quite ludicrously, given the situation—disappointment.

She bit her lip, eyes dropping away from his face, and thus not seeing the way something flared in the dark grey depths of his eyes. When her gaze went back to him his expression was bland once more.

He was a businessman, she realised. He was wearing a business suit, very smart, very formal. And very respectable.

He's just offered to go round the cathedral with you, that's all. He's not asking for a night of torrid sex, for heaven's sake! And he's proved he can keep all those pests away from you…

She took a breath, and lifted her chin.

'Thank you,' she said. 'That would be very kind.'

Markos glanced down at the glorious red-gold head averted from him, focused on whatever the audio guide was describing to her. It was a novelty to have something compete with him for a woman's attention, especially a medieval cathedral. But then, the girl's concentration on the glories of the interior of Nôtre Dame was allowing him to concentrate on her own glories.

And they were remarkable.

She really was, he mused as they made their slow way around the cathedral, quite exquisite. Everything—from the fantastic sunburst of her hair, the tender line of her throat, the delicate curve of her cheek, the silken translucence of her skin, to the unconscious grace of her slender, yet shapely body—was exquisite. And that she seemed unconscious of it was enticing all on its own. She seemed to have no idea just how beautiful she was. A wry smile quirked at Markos's lips. Was the girl mad to walk out in Paris, of all cities, with her breathtaking looks, and then be surprised that she was a honeypot to every male around? Including, he thought cynically, himself.

A self-mocking expression fleeted in his face. Picking up females on the street was not something he made a habit of, not even to stave off boredom. But... His eyes wandered over her again as she stared, face lifted, at the radiance of the rose window. For a beauty so exquisite, so unselfconscious, he was definitely prepared to make an exception.

His gaze moved on downwards, taking in her tall, slender figure, the beautiful swell of her breasts, her narrow waist and hips and her long legs. Even in the chainstore clothes she was wearing she was exceptional. As to what she would look like properly gowned—Markos let his imagination play pleasurably over how much her beauty would be enhanced by couture clothes.

And jewellery, of course. Paris boasted some of the best jewellers in the world, but if he wanted something special for the girl he knew just where to turn. His cousin, Leo Makarios, had just informed him—as smug as you like, thought Markos—that he had become the owner of a fabulous cache of Tsarist jewels, come to light in the former Soviet Union. Surely something amongst the treasure trove of the Levantsky collection would be suitable to adorn the rare beauty of the woman at his side.

Sapphires or emeralds? Markos gave his imagination free rein, visualising her freely bedecked in jewellery of each stone. Or both.

He would enjoy, very much, discovering which suited her best.

As he would enjoy, very much, discovering all her beauty in his bed.

Satisfaction and a pleasurable anticipation eased through him. Suddenly, thanks to this extraordinarily beautiful girl, life had become a lot more interesting. His *ennui* had vanished entirely.

Vanessa craned her neck upwards at the glorious fractured rainbow pouring through the interstices of the fretworked rose window. The narrative in her ears was telling her dates and monarchs, and the technicalities of producing medieval stained glass, but though she was listening as attentively as she could, the guide had a formidable distraction.

A distraction who kept making her want to swivel her eyes to him and check whether he really was as breathtaking as she thought he was. But, although the temptation was very great, she forced herself to resist. She had to. She was here to see Paris, nothing more.

She had promised herself this trip after her grandfather had died in the spring, finally succumbing to the long decline in health that had started when her grandmother had died so unexpectedly three years ago, knowing she would need to have something to focus on during her bereavement.

Familiar grief pierced through her. Her grandparents had brought her up since the tragic death of her parents in a car crash when she had been too young to remember them. But though her grandparents had been caring and loving, they had also been over-protective. For their sakes she had repressed her adolescent yearnings and restlessness. When she was a child, her grandparents had been her life, her safety—as a young adult, she had become theirs. She could not abandon them.

So she had forgone much of what girls of her age seized with eagerness. She had contented herself with studying librarianship at her local college, instead of art or languages at a distant university, so she could continue to live with her grandparents in their comfortable Victorian house in the pleasant town in the south of England where she'd always lived. Instead of travelling the world in the vacations she had worked in the local library as an assistant, reading books about faraway places rather than visiting them with backpack and boots. And instead of parties and clubbing and boyfriends she had taken her grandparents to the local theatre, to see classical plays and nostalgia concerts.

It had been a life frozen in time, sedate and confined, but she had not begrudged it. She had known, after all, with a dull pain in her heart, that it would not last for ever. Her grandmother's death had been sudden, her grandfather's protracted, his decline such that she had given up her work at the library to nurse him, restricting her life even further. But she had known she must make the very most of loving them, and being loved, while she still had them.

And now they were both gone, and she had all the time in the world for herself. It was freedom, but tinged with sadness, knowing she was alone in the world, with no one at home for her any longer.

Yet, for all her haunting sadness, she could not help the fizz of excitement that had bubbled perpetually through her veins since she had arrived at the airport to take her budget airline flight to Paris. Everything had seemed wonderful, enchanting, exciting—taking the Metro, trying out her French on real Parisians, walking, open-mouthed, through the streets with her hand luggage to the old-fashioned little *pension* tucked away in a small side street on the Right Bank. She was determined to see everything she could fit in.

Starting with Nôtre Dame. She had seen the great cathedral like a ship in sail in the River Seine and made a beeline for it.

Just as every male in Paris had seemed instantly to make a beeline for *her.*

Frustration nipped through her again. Why couldn't they leave her alone? She wasn't the slightest bit interested, but she just couldn't shake them off! It was exasperating, threatening to spoil her visit.

Her eyes flickered sideways from the carvings above the arches that the audio guide was drawing her attention to.

She wasn't being pestered now, though. The man at her side was seeing to that. And he, thank heavens, was not trying to pester her either!

If he did, would it be pestering?

The rogue thought wandered into her mind. She crushed it at once, but it had done its damage. Something she had read somewhere came to her. *It's only harassment if you don't fancy them...*

Cynical, yes, but it had some truth to it.

And the man at her side was, she had to admit, incredibly fanciable, by any woman's demanding standards...

She gave herself a mental shake. He'd simply offered to keep the pests off her, nothing more! He was just being a good compatriot, that was all. Protecting her from all those 'foreign johnnies'. A smile tugged at her mouth at his gentle mockery of traditional British xenophobia.

I wonder what nationality he is other than English?

Covertly, her eyes flickered to him again, just for an instant. He was gazing along the length of the chancel, towards the altar, and did not see her look at him. She was glad. She could not, after all, feel anything other than awkward about this whole thing. If it hadn't been for the pests she would never have been walking around Nôtre Dame with a complete stranger as a bodyguard!

Her stolen glance gave her no more illumination other than Mediterranean. He really could have been anything. Oh, well, it was none of her business anyway. And any moment now the guide would end, and she would thank him politely, and off he would go, his good deed done for the day.

She would never see him again.

* * *

'All done?'

The girl was taking off her headphones, clicking the audio machine to off. She nodded in reply to Markos's enquiry.

'Yes. Isn't it the most amazing place?' Her voice was breathy, eyes shining. They were like pools of gold, he thought.

She went on speaking. 'I was worried it might not be as wonderful as everyone says, but it is! The rose window is just unbelievable! And I love the way they've painted the ceilings in the chapel—apparently in the Middle Ages they painted lots of the stonework, which seems a bit strange to our eyes. But of course I expect you've seen it lots of times before—'

She broke off, as if conscious of running on, and made a business of putting the audio guide away.

'Not for many years. And one thing I've never done,' he went on, making his voice sound ruminative, 'is go up into the towers. I always meant to.' His eyes flickered down at her, meeting hers briefly as she glanced up at him, open surprise in her face. He smiled. 'Were you planning on making the ascent?'

He could see her swallow. 'Well, yes. I was going to, actually.' She sounded a bit awkward, and still delightfully breathy. Markos felt that spear of satisfaction go through him again. She might have paid scrupulous attention to her audio guide, but now she was very much back to being aware of him.

Just the way he wanted her to be.

'Good.' His voice was smooth as butter. 'Well, what are we waiting for?'

She looked blank for a moment. He quizzed an eyebrow at her. 'The entrance to the towers is around the side—from the outside, I believe.' He started to usher her towards the cathedral's exit. Automatically she moved forward, as he directed.

Once back out in the warm bright sunshine again, he saw her pause and start to turn. She was going to say something very English, and polite, and dismissive, he could see.

So he gave her no chance to do so.

'This way,' he said, and ushered her forward again, heading sideways across the arched west face.

'Um…' said the girl.

He smiled. A courteous, civil smile, that he might bestow on a fifty-year-old female. Nothing like the kind of smile he would direct at a woman he found desirable.

It had the effect he'd intended. She subsided into compliance.

There was, Markos could see, as he gained the north side of the cathedral, a slight queue to gain entrance to the towers. He ushered the girl into the last place, and stood behind her.

'It shouldn't be long,' he said, giving her another brief, courteous, civil smile. 'Do please excuse me a moment.'

He slid a long-fingered hand inside his jacket pocket and took out his mobile. From the corner of his eye he could see Taki and Stelios, who had emerged from the cathedral where they had been assiduously shadowing him, and punched their number. When Taki answered he spoke briefly in Greek, telling him to cancel his lunch appointment, give Monsieur Dubois suitable apologies and say he would be happy to call on him at his convenience to make amends. Then he cut the connection and replaced his mobile.

The girl was looking at him, a slightly curious expression in her eyes.

'Greek,' elucidated Markos, guessing what her question was.

'I wondered what the other half of you was!' she exclaimed.

He smiled. This time it was distinctly *not* the smile he'd give to a fifty-year-old female. He saw her expression change, deep in those lustrous amber eyes, and the shaft of satisfaction went through him again.

'Greek father, English mother,' he told her.

'You don't look at all English. What part of Greece do you come from?'

Markos thought of the dozen homes he'd had since a child—half of them in England and anywhere else in Europe that was fashionable—with his mother as she fought her interminable divorce battle with his father, and wondered which one would qualify as the part of Greece he came from. He'd never felt particularly at home in any of them.

Or anywhere.

So he gave the answer he always gave instead.

'My family originally came from Turkey, one of the many Greek communities there. In the nineteen twenties my great-grandfather settled in Athens. But these days—' he smiled at her, his eyes privately washing over her '—I am footloose, calling nowhere home. Ah, the queue is moving at last.'

He was glad to change the subject. Home was not a word that had meaning to him.

'More coffee?'

Vanessa shook her head. 'No, thank you.' She looked hesitant a moment, then said, 'Um, I really ought to go.'

She was sitting under an awning outside a restaurant in a little square close to Nôtre Dame. Quite how she had ended up having lunch here she still wasn't sure. It just seemed to have happened, she thought, bemused.

Markos Makarios. That was his name. He'd introduced himself on the topmost portion of the tower that they'd climbed up to, with all of Paris at their feet.

'Now you'll always associate me with the Hunchback of Nôtre Dame.' He'd smiled at her, a teasing light in those dark, slate-grey eyes, the eyes she kept wanting to gaze into but knew she mustn't.

Just as she should not have given her own name in return, or let him shake hands with her in mock solemnity, on the rooftop of Nôtre Dame, in the warm September sunshine, sliding her fingers into his strong, lean grip.

And she certainly should not have allowed herself, on their descent, to have her elbow taken, as though it were the most natural thing in the world, be strolled off across the *parvis*, and be informed that it was time for lunch by Markos Makarios, who was, despite his kindness in removing pests from her, still a stranger.

But somehow she had.

'To Paris—and to your enjoyment of it.' Markos lifted his glass to toast her, and she smiled back at him, and just for the merest moment something glinted in his eyes—something very deep, very brief—and a frisson went through her that had nothing to do with the wonder of being here in Paris, eating lunch in a little square on the Ile de la Cité, under an awning, surrounded by other Parisiens attending to that most important of all French pastimes: the consumption of beautifully cooked food.

But then the glint was gone, and the frisson was once again nothing more than the wonder of Paris itself.

Nothing to do with the man who, for some reason she could not quite explain, was having lunch with her.

It's only lunch. That's all. He's just being polite. Civil. Kind. Friendly. Taking pity on an English tourist in Paris for the first time.

And who still had a busy itinerary ahead of her for the day.

She started to free her shoulder bag, secured by one of the chair legs—she could not afford to be careless with her belongings—and lifted it up on to her lap, delving into the interior for her wallet.

'Would you be kind enough to ask for separate bills?' she said.

Markos looked at her. He had wanted novelty—now he'd got it. No woman of his entire acquaintance had ever made even a token objection to his paying for her lunch, or anything else.

'I will take care of that,' he said dismissively, and beckoned the waiter. Normally he would have left such mundane details to Taki or Stelios, but they were seated in the square, apparently reading newspapers. Vanessa had not noticed them.

Vanessa. He played the name around in his mind. She had had to give it to him when he'd told her his. And that was another source of novelty. Women were usually extremely keen to be on first-name terms with him as soon as possible—hoping for more than the mere intimacy of names. This pre-Raphaelite beauty had seemed almost reluctant to give her name.

Almost shy.

His eyes flickered over her.

And yet she'd had lunch with him. He could see, with some amusement, that she wasn't sure how that had come about. There was a faintly bemused look in her face, as though she could not really believe she had done it. Though it amused him, it also pleased him.

It was rare to find a woman who wasn't all over him like a rash.

But then, Vanessa Ovington was a rare find indeed.

One he would enjoy—relish—to the full.

The waiter appeared, and Markos slipped out his wallet, handing the man one of his cards. Hurriedly Vanessa fumbled for some euro notes, and pushed them across the table.

'I think that covers my share,' she said.

Markos looked blankly at her. There was, he could see, a glint in those golden eyes. A sudden smile tugged at his mouth.

'Thank you,' he said smoothly, and took the notes. 'Sometimes it is a case of *reculer pour mieux sauter.*'

It was Vanessa's turn to look blank.

'To retreat in order the better to advance,' Markos translated.

She still looked blank. Clearly she had no idea why he had said what he had.

But Markos did not mind. He did not mind at all.

There was one very clear destination to which he was advancing, and that this exquisite redhead did not yet seem to realise it only added a piquancy that was as pleasurable as it was novel.

'Now,' he said urbanely, 'where shall we go? Les Invalides or the Rodin museum? You said you couldn't decide which to see first.'

Somehow—and Vanessa really couldn't work out how afterwards, even though she thought about it and thought about it—she went with him, as meekly as a lamb.

CHAPTER TWO

IT TOOK HIM a week to get her to bed. He did not rush it. Indeed, the novelty of her company was such that he savoured the slow, leisurely seduction. Not that she was aware of it— and that, as ever, added its own piquancy. That first afternoon he had taken her to the Musée de Rodin, taking pleasure in watching her make her slow, absorbed way among the works of France's greatest sculptor.

He'd watched her gaze, awestruck, at the famous *Le Penseur* in the museum grounds, the sunlight playing on the red-gold of her tumbled pre-Raphaelite locks. No sculptor could catch that, he'd thought. Even paint on canvas would be inadequate—stiff and lifeless. Her hair was almost a living thing, and he'd wanted to spear his fingers through it, draw her face towards him, lift her mouth to his, taste the bounty of her parted lips...

A leaf had fluttered down from one of the overhanging trees, catching in her mane of hair.

'Hold still,' he'd instructed softly.

She had halted, half twisting her head up towards him. Deftly his fingers had freed the trapped leaf and sent it spinning down to the path. Yet he had not released her, one hand resting on her shoulder, one still held against her hair. For one long moment he had luxuriated in the way she was looking up at him.

The lustrous, amber eyes gazing helplessly up at him had been rich with emotions—part afraid, part tantalised, part bewildered—and he had been able to tell with every experienced sinew of his body, part dawning with the awareness that was quivering through her.

For that long moment, in the dappled sunlight, in the afternoon warmth, there had been a stillness netting them. At the very edge of his consciousness, Markos had felt something stir. Something quite alien to him.

He had not known what it was.

What he had known, with a sure and certain knowledge, was that he was about to embark on an affair that would banish his *ennui* very, very effectively.

And that, right then, was exactly what he'd wanted.

As the days had unfolded his certainty had been confirmed. Vanessa Ovington was different from any other woman he had pursued. Not just because she was so completely unaware of being pursued, not just because she seemed to be genuinely interested in seeing the sights of Paris, around which he escorted her assiduously—from the Eiffel Tower and the Arc de Triomphe to the splendours of Versailles and the Sacré Coeur and everything in between—not just because she kept insisting on paying her share of entrance tickets and restaurant bills—an insistence that amused him so much that he continued to banish Taki and Stelios and resort to taxis instead of his customary limo, and he made no attempt to take her to any of Paris's fabled couture houses and lavish on her the wealth she seemed to have neither inkling of nor interest in—but because…because…

It wasn't something he found he could quite put into words—either in English or in Greek. Vanessa was different, that was all—and her difference intrigued and fascinated him almost as much as her beauty captivated him.

And on the night that he finally brought his leisurely

pursuit to its inevitable conclusion he discovered something else about her that was quite unique in his experience of women.

She came willingly to his apartment, situated in a fashionable Right Bank *arrondissement*. She was in no state of mind by then to do otherwise, and like someone in a dream she let him lead her inside. Her eyes widened as she took in the rich interior, but she said nothing. He was not surprised. In the time they had spent together she had shown absolutely no interest in discovering the state of his wealth. So far as she was concerned, he concluded, he was merely a businessman—what his business was, or whether it was lucrative or not, she had never asked. A single enquiry by her the first time he took her to dinner had been more for politeness than anything else, and when he'd replied, 'Oh, import and export,' she'd simply nodded vaguely and left it at that. She'd clearly never heard of the Makarios Corporation, let alone that it was worth several billion euros, or that he was owner of a substantial portion of it.

But if she were indifferent to whether he was rich or not, she was not, he knew, indifferent to *him*. Day after day, in his slow, leisurely seduction, he had been making her more and more aware of him—of his desire for her. But he had done so with infinite slowness, infinite care. She was not a woman to rush; she was a woman to bring, step by step, to this point in time where, at last, after longer than he had ever had to wait for a woman—another source of pleasurable novelty—he would finally taste her sweetness to the full.

As she stood gazing around the opulent apartment, her eyes widening as she took in an Impressionist painting on the wall—clearly assuming, Markos noted with suppressed amusement, that it was a mere copy, not the priceless original it really was—he strolled across to the eighteenth-century cabinet that had been converted to a modern drinks cabinet inside, and took out a chilled bottle of vintage champagne.

The soft pop of the cork startled her.

'Oh,' she mouthed, her eyes widening still more as he approached her with a pair of foaming glasses. She took the long flute gingerly as he proffered it to her.

'I already drank wine over dinner,' she said.

'Champagne cannot make you drunk.' Markos smiled. 'It's far too exquisite to have anything coarse in its effects.'

She looked at him uncertainly. Markos tilted his glass against hers a moment, then lifted his towards his lips.

'To us, Vanessa,' he said softly.

She did not drink. Only stood there, her hair like a living flame around her head, cascading over her shoulders in the simple pale green frock she wore, her eyes wide and lambent.

Nor did she speak, only gazed at him, her eyes as eloquent as her voice was not, telling him, as if he needed to know, that she was his—his for the touching, the taking, the possessing.

'Taste the champagne, Vanessa,' he said, even more softly.

Obediently, she raised the glass to her lips and took a small, hesitant mouthful, then lowered her glass again. She was still gazing at him helplessly, mutely.

'And now taste me,' he murmured, and as he spoke he lowered his head to her and at last, after so many days, did what he had wanted to do the first moment of seeing her.

Touch and taste the sweet honey of her lips.

He felt them tremble beneath his own as he grazed them softly, felt them ripen, it seemed, as with the merest tip of his tongue he touched them. She trembled again, in her whole body, the finest quiver shimmering through her, and he heard the softest sigh in her throat.

'Vanessa,' he breathed, and at the slight parting of his lips to say her name he parted hers as well, and tasted her finally—finally to the full.

His kiss was long and deep and leisurely. Exploring all the

sweetness, all the nectar of her mouth. The moment was exquisite, and he savoured it.

Without her realising it he had deposited his champagne flute and then relieved her of hers, and now, hands untrammelled, he drew her soft, slender body against his.

He felt the quiver come again, vibrating through her as his arms slid around her, moulding her pliant body to him. The swell of her breasts against him shot its own tremor through him, and he felt his body surge.

His kiss deepened, turning from exploration to desire, quickening its own appetite.

He gave her no time to speak, no time to utter the bemusement he knew was sweeping through her as he swept her up into the plane of sensuous existence he was already occupying.

His hands slid up along her spine, spearing into the glorious tresses of her hair. He felt himself quicken, his sweet plunder of her mouth deepen. A low, soft moan escaped her, and he felt her lean more against him, the ripening swell of her breasts pressing him.

He was full and ready for her, but she, he knew, was not ready. He could tell from the bemused wideness of her eyes that she was bewildered by what was happening to her, that he was taking her to a place without her conscious realisation. Yet her body was taking her; each quivering reaction to his touch, his caress, was bringing her closer. Now all that was needed was to wake her to what was happening to her.

He drew back a little, easing from her, and gazed down at her. Her lips were parted, like sweet ripe strawberries, and her pupils distended and huge.

He drew a single finger down her cheek, feeling her quiver. She could not speak, was beyond speech, and it pleased him with a deep, primitive pleasure that this exquisite creature should be so helpless to his touch.

His finger drew across her mouth, feeling the gliding

moistness he had aroused, and then continued down the tender
line of her throat to graze the now straining swell of her
breast, cupped in its simple bodice. He drew the material
down with him, hearing the soft, shocked intake of her breath
as her swelling breast was displayed for him.

A soft murmur of Greek escaped him, speaking of ripeness
and sweetness and beauty. For a moment he simply looked
at the exquisite bared breast, and then, his lashes sweeping
down over his eyes, he lowered his head to her.

He felt the peak harden in his mouth as he drew on it.
Heard again the low, shocked, helpless moan sound in her
throat. Felt her hand lift and touch his hair, trembling. He
drew again on the ripe succulence, teasing it between his lips,
and felt her trembling increase, the low moan of shock and
pleasure come again. His body hardened more, blood surging
in him. His teeth closed over her, grazing at her, sending, he
knew, shooting, sensual flares through her that made her
moan again, made her fingers tremble in his hair…

When he released her, taking one last long caress of his
tongue to do so, he did not hesitate. He swept her up into his
arms, glorying in the closeness of her body cupped against
him. Her arms wound about his neck as he carried her.

'Markos—' Her voice was low, and breathless, and her
eyes were wide with bemusement still, but more than that—
with a longing in them, a desire for him that she could no
longer hide, but which feasted on him, gazing up at him.

And she continued to gaze helplessly up at him as he
lowered her down on the silken covers of his bed, as he
shrugged off with rapid, practised fingers the clothes that
were now nothing more than an impediment, and then as
he came to her where she lay, her hair a living flame, her
body indenting the softness of the pillowed bed, one ripe,
rounded breast displayed for him, the hem of her dress
riding up over one thigh.

His breath caught even as his body surged. God, but she was exquisite, beautiful, the image of desire.

And yet not wanton. There was an innocence in her unconscious, helpless sensuousness that speared through him as she gazed up at him, the longing, the yearning, the bemusement rich in her gaze.

Slowly he came down beside her, fingers brushing the hair like an aureole around her beautiful face.

He heard her speak, wonder and disbelief in her voice.

'Is this a dream? Is this really happening?'

A smile parted his lips, and he lowered his mouth slowly to hers.

'No dream,' he assured her.

He tasted once more the sweet nectar of her mouth, and then, with infinite patience, infinite pleasure, moved on to taste the sweetness of all her body—her milky rounded breasts, their ripe and straining peaks that he teased and flamed with lips and tongue and teeth, her silken flanks, the slender moulding of her hips, the slim length of her legs that he smoothed and caressed. And then his hands caressed her soft thighs apart, to seek and find the secret satin flesh between, that made the low gasps in her throat come again and again as his skilled, gliding fingers drew from her the honeydew of her aching pleasure until she was trembling and straining beneath him, her body arching to his as he readied her for his possession. The soft moans she gave, the glistening ripeness of her silky folds, the yielding contours of her body, all told him that now, *now* she was at the moment of his long-awaited fulfilment of his desire, and he lifted himself over her.

For one long, last, exquisite moment he denied himself, and then no more.

With slow, absolute possession he filled her.

And discovered, when it was far, far too late to do anything other than reap the exquisite fulfilment of everything he had wanted of this extraordinarily alluring girl, that he was the first to taste that ultimate sweetness.

'Are…are you angry with me?'

Her voice was so tentative, so diffident, it made him tense a moment.

Her face shadowed. 'I should have told you,' she said quietly, her voice stricken.

Something in it, in the expression in her eyes, stabbed at him. If, ten minutes ago, anyone should have asked him if he'd wanted to take a virgin to bed, he'd have given a short, unequivocal answer. No.

But now—

He looked down at her as she lay beneath him.

His breath caught. She was so beautiful—just so beautiful.

But it was more than beauty—he didn't know what it was, but it was there. There in the wide, clouding eyes—something that reached to him. He did not know what, or how; he only knew, with sudden, absolute certainty that he did not care that she had been a virgin. It simply did not matter. All that mattered was that she was as different from the women he bedded as a glittering diamond from a hidden pearl. That was her allure. That she was like no woman he had ever possessed.

And when the moment of full possession had come, after the momentary shock of realising just how inexperienced she was, when his body had surged within hers and the last vestige of consciousness had been drowned in a tide of sensation that had swept over them both, as he'd known from the sudden clenching of her body around him, from the cry that had come from her throat, the taut arching of her neck, the blaze of shocked, incandescent awareness in her eyes—then he had experienced a pleasure so exceptional, so rare, so complete that it had consumed him, searing through him like a brand, sating him so that he knew he had never before felt anything as intense, as absolute as this, with any woman.

That strange, unknown emotion reached to him as she lay gazing up at him, her expression shadowed and anxious, welling through him again.

He drew himself down to her, entwining her body with his, holding her close to him, feeling the softness of her body, the sweetness of it in his arms. And he knew with that same certainty that he had made exactly the right decision when he had followed his impulse that day outside Nôtre Dame.

He kissed her softly, on her mouth and on her eyes.

'You were perfect,' he told her, his voice low and husky. 'Quite, quite perfect.'

As he lifted his head away and gazed down smiling at her, he saw her face light up as if the sun had come out in her eyes—a radiance that filled her being.

It pleased him.

Pleased him very much.

CHAPTER THREE

THE SNOW WAS crisp beneath Vanessa's ski boots, the air crystalline in her lungs. She stood at the foot of the piste, gazing anxiously up the steep mountain slope, already shadowing at the end of the Alpine winter's afternoon. Almost beyond her vision she could see a dot moving, dark against the glittering snow, heading downwards in swift, powerful sweeps.

Anxiety bit at her, and she had to force herself to be calm. Markos was a superb skier, she knew that, and he could handle a run of this severity with ease. But her novice eyes saw only the plummeting drop, the deadly rocky outcrops, the hairpin turns.

Please let him be all right!

The plea was automatic, urgent. If anything happened to Markos she would die.

As she watched with bated breath, him drawing closer to her, she found herself wondering yet again how it was that this extraordinary miracle had occurred.

How could she ever have thought, the morning she went out to explore Paris for the very first time, that her life would change for ever on that very day? She had not known it—not that first day, nor any of the magical days that followed—until that wondrous fairytale night when he had swept her away and made her his.

And then she had known, completely and utterly, with a certainty that had flooded through her, consuming her and possessing her and overwhelming her.

She was in love.

In love with the most wonderful man in the world.

She had never been in love before. How could she have? She had lived at home, quietly and sedately, occasionally going out with young men she worked with, or friends of friends—men who were safe, that her grandparents had felt her to be safe with. She had experienced some kisses, nothing more. Nothing to make her want more, nothing to melt her like ice in a searing flame the way Markos's kisses melted her, the way his touch inflamed her, the way his eyes caressed her, his arms held her, his body possessed her.

She felt weakness flooding through her just thinking of him. And wonder—above all, wonder.

He chose me—from all the women he could choose from, he chose me!

Every day, every night, the miracle that that choice had brought about for her consumed her. She had been chosen by the man she adored.

She still could not really understand why. Now that she knew his lifestyle, where he could have anything and anyone he wanted, it made it all the more miraculous that he was so content with her.

And she was content just to be with him. Wanting nothing else. The past had ceased to exist, and the future too. Nothing existed for her except the perpetual now of being with Markos, only with Markos. Going where he went, doing what he wanted, being what he wanted.

Nothing else existed.

Only Markos—and his wanting her, and her loving him so much, so very much...

He filled her world.

And it was enough—oh, more than enough. It was everything to her.

He slewed to a snow-spraying halt in front of her, jabbing his ski poles deep into the snow and lifting his visor. His eyes went to her immediately.

'Did you think I'd kill myself?' he asked, a grin dazzling in his face.

Numbly she nodded, sick with relief that he had made his descent of the black run safely.

He gave a laugh for answer. 'You'll be doing black runs yourself soon,' he told her, removing his helmet and shaking out his dark hair.

Vanessa paled.

'Oh, no, I couldn't—really.'

He laughed again, handing his helmet across to Taki, who had stepped forward to take it.

'How was your lesson?'

She made a face. 'Poor Christian was very polite, but he knows I'm useless.'

Markos's dark eyes glinted. 'Would you prefer another instructor?'

Vanessa looked rueful. 'It's not the teacher that's the problem—it's the pupil, I'm afraid.'

The laugh came again, as Markos stooped to unlatch his skis and step free. He left them where they were for Taki to sort out, and wrapped an arm around Vanessa's shoulder.

'Perhaps I should give you personal lessons.' His head bent lower. 'After all, I've been a good teacher in other respects, no?'

There was a huskiness in his voice that brought colour flaring out along her cheeks. The sight of it never failed to amuse Markos. Though she had been with him for five months, she could still be astonishingly reserved. Even a casual comment like this, reminding her of how much he had taught her about sexual pleasure, could bring it on. Not that he objected. It was one of the reasons she still continued to have such intense charms for him—the novelty of having a mistress who was so entirely unlike any other had still not yet worn off.

Nor were there any signs of it doing so.

He walked towards the waiting Jeep, his arm still around her shoulder. Both of them were padded with ski-jackets, and her body seemed frustratingly buried. The hard, demanding run had been exhilarating, storming him with the adrenaline needed to handle it, and he knew exactly what he wanted next. The twenty-minute drive down to the *schloss* would be punishingly long.

Once there, though, he would whisk Vanessa up to their suite, the damn ski jackets would hit the floor and that vast monstrosity of a four-poster bed could justify its existence.

He shook his head as he climbed into the Jeep after Vanessa. His cousin Leo must have been nuts to buy that place! He'd spent a fortune doing it up, but the best plan would have been to turn it into a hotel, not a private residence. Still, he mused, that was his cousin all over—making grand gestures, just like he was doing now, inviting the world and his wife to this razzmatazz launch of the Levantsky collection of Tsarist jewels.

Markos's eyes wandered to Vanessa. She'd thrown back the hood of her ski-jacket, unzipping it in the warmth of the Jeep, and yet again Markos was struck by her beauty.

How the hell had he been the first to possess her? It still astounded him to think about it. Most English girls lost their virginity early, yet Vanessa had been untouched at twenty-four. But, as he'd found out about her hitherto restricted life, he'd realised that she had simply never had the opportunity.

But with him—oh, she had opportunity all right. Opportunity, and the total inability to resist him! She had gone to his bed without the slightest demur, the slightest hesitation, had gone with ardour, melting into his embrace, accepting his caresses, breathless beneath his kisses, yielding to him absolutely, completely, consumingly.

Perfect, he had called her—and she was. Completely perfect for him.

Possessiveness flared through him, powerful and potent. He had set his seal on her and she was his.

And she basked in it, he could tell. Even now, after five months together, her face still lit when he came up to her. Every time. Oh, his cousin Leo could be as cynical as he liked, but what did that signify? A mocking smile came to his mouth as he compared Vanessa to the sable-haired beauty whom Leo had his eye on, and who was giving him such a hard time. That was Leo's problem. As for himself, right now life was just fine. And having Vanessa gazing up at him with that bemused, adoring expression on her face was a good, good feeling.

He waited impatiently as Taki finished loading the ski-gear onto the roof of the Jeep and climbed in beside Stelios in the driver's seat. The engine revved and they moved off slowly over the snowy trackway.

He turned to Vanessa.

'Is all the photography finally over now?'

She nodded. 'Yes, thank goodness.'

A frown drew his eyebrows together. 'You did not enjoy it?'

There was a guarded note in his voice, and Vanessa bit her lip. It had been entirely Markos's idea that she should be the fourth model for his cousin Leo to use to publicise the Levantsky jewellery collection. Her objections that she had never modelled in her life had been swept aside. So had her observation that the photographer might prefer to work with a professional model, not some amateur.

Both cousins had looked at her, blank expression on their faces. They were so similar, clearly related to each other, and yet Leo Makarios, for all his broad shoulders and heavily sensual looks, could have been a block of stone so far as she was concerned. It was Markos, with his powerful build, his fine-cut features, the humour lurking at his mouth and the way his grey eyes could suddenly flare with naked desire, who held her in thrall. Who twisted her heart until it was a knot inside her breast. Who sent her heart-rate soaring, her breathing haywire, her body trembling and weak.

She knew now what that shared blank look had meant. It had meant that the very idea that the preferences of someone paid to work for Leo Makarios should be taken into account simply did not exist for either of the cousins. It was an attitude that had, at first, astonished her.

But then, the realisation of just who she had fallen in love with still seemed quite unbelievable. She could remember the moment when it had dawned. It had been the afternoon of their first time together. They had arisen, finally, after spending most of the day still in bed, and Markos had smiled down at her, and told her they should start getting ready to go to the opera.

'Is it Wagner?' she had asked tentatively, because his were the only operas she knew that were so long they started in the afternoon.

He'd only shaken his head and laughed.

'Far more romantic,' he'd assured her.

It had been. And more than just romantic.

Utterly, devastatingly eye-opening.

She had emerged from the bathroom to find the bedroom swarming with people, all chattering away in French. For the next hour she had been at their mercy—having her hair cut and styled, her nails manicured, her body measurements taken, her face made up and one incredible gown after another draped over her. And then, finally, when she had stood, bemused and more beautiful than she had ever looked in her life, wearing a gold tissue gown and a golden torque around her throat, Markos had walked in, taking her breath away as she gazed at him in his tuxedo, and smiled at her.

'Come,' he had said to her. 'Your chariot awaits, Cinderella.'

But it hadn't been a chariot, nor even a limo.

It had been a private jet, and they had flown to Milan, to take in *La Bohème* at La Scala, and for the first time Vanessa had realised that the man she had fallen in love with was no ordinary businessman.

He was one of the richest men in Europe.

The discovery—which had at first overwhelmed her—had made her realise over again just how miraculous it was that Markos should have chosen *her* to be with him.

He could have any woman he wants—but he wants me.

It was a warm glow around her heart.

But it brought its difficulties, all the same. The rich, she had swiftly discovered, really were different. They saw life not as ordinary people saw it, and treated others differently from themselves. Markos was never rude to anyone, yet there was, Vanessa had swiftly become aware, an intransigence about him. What he wanted, he got. Not by demands, or petulance, or bad behaviour. He got it because…well, because he was Markos Makarios. People did what he wanted. Staff, servants—everyone.

Even her.

Unease skittered through her mind. No, she did what Markos wanted because she *wanted* to do what he wanted. How could she possibly want to do anything else? She loved him, adored him; he was everything to her—everything! She would walk over broken glass for him. Not that he would ever ask her to.

Now, as his brows drew together, evincing displeasure at the very thought that she might not have enjoyed being a model, she knew that he would never subject her to something she did not want. Entirely the opposite! He had showered her with his largesse, lavishing his wealth on her. And far, far more than his wealth.

Himself.

That was what melted her heart, warmed her like a living flame. That he spent his time with her, took her with him wherever he went, showing her all the wonderful far-away places she'd only ever dreamt of, kept her at his side by day and by night, except when work took him away as it must, inevitably, when he was running half of a business empire as vast as the Makarios Corporation.

'We run it between us, Leo and I,' Markos had told her, when she had first realised just what his true circumstances were. 'His father—my uncle—is dead, and mine is retired now, so Leo and I have it to ourselves so far as executive power is concerned.'

'Don't you ever argue?' she had asked, half curious, half teasing.

Markos had shrugged, humour pulling at his mouth.

'Oh, big cousin Leo likes to think he gets his own way, but I see him off when I have to.'

When she had met Leo she had seen that the relationship between them worked well. Though cut from similar cloth— both with scarily sharp business minds, both as rich as each other—Markos had the cooler head, Leo was swifter to anger. Markos was more calculating, Leo more impulsive. True, Leo liked to make Markos recognise his place as the younger of the two, but he also, she could see, had both respect and fondness for him.

A frown crossed her brow. Leo had spent the evening of the launch gala with one of the models—Anna—clamped to his side. Anna hadn't seemed very happy about it, but then she wasn't very happy about the shoot anyway. Vanessa wasn't surprised—Anna had clashed with the horrible photographer, who had done nothing but shout at them all day.

Now, with Markos asking her if she had enjoyed it, she could—knowing it was finally all over—be honest.

'Not really,' she confessed. 'I don't think it's my thing, really—modelling.'

'You looked fantastic.'

'It's harder work than you think,' Vanessa answered. 'I hadn't realised what a strain it would be. I know you think it's just posing in gorgeous clothes, wearing fabulous necklaces and things, but you get so tired. And Signor Embrutti was very demanding. He was rather unpleasant, actually.'

Markos's expression was thunderous. 'To you? You should have walked out. Come and told me.'

'No! Honestly, it was fine. If anything he was less horrible to me than any of the other girls. Because everyone knows that you and I—' She fell silent again.

Markos nodded. 'That is as well,' he said grimly, and reached for her hand. She squeezed his fingers, seeking to lighten the atmosphere, glancing out for inspiration over the darkening snow-covered landscape they were driving through.

'When did you learn to ski?' she asked.

'God knows,' he replied, easing back in the seat. 'My mother skied and she took me wherever she went, so I suppose I was pretty young.'

'Did she teach you?' Vanessa's face broke into a smile, seeing a miniature Markos lovingly helped to ski by a doting mother. It was a rare glimpse of the man behind the lover.

'No, she hired instructors.'

His face shuttered. The last thing his mother would have bothered with was teaching him to ski. Not only had she been too busy with her lover *du jour* up in a mountain lodge somewhere private, but the only reason she had lugged her son around with her everywhere had been to make sure she kept him safely. He was, after all, her prime asset, and he had to be kept secure.

Vanessa saw his expression close and changed the subject, knowing she must not feel snubbed. Markos never talked about his family—except for his cousin Leo—and she respected his privacy. After all, he did not talk to her about her family. When he had swept her off with him she had simply told him that her parents had died when she was young, and that the grandparents who had raised her had both died, so she was a free agent. He had only smiled glintingly down at her, said 'Not any more, Vanessa,' and kissed her, deeply and possessively, taking her mind very effectively off anything other than himself—and the wonderful, magical implications of what he had just said to her.

Now, casting about for something innocuous to say, she asked, 'Is that the Dorf below the castle? I can see lights through the trees.'

Markos glanced out of the window. 'Probably. God knows what possessed Leo to buy that white elephant! It's as well he didn't do so under corporate finances, or I'd have lambasted him for it! It can be his own personal money pit if he wants.'

'It *is* very big,' Vanessa allowed.

The glint in Markos's eyes came again, its message very clear. He leant towards her, lips brushing hers.

'Even better, the beds are very big too, hmm?'

There was a softness in his voice, a husk of anticipation. Once again, colour flared out across her cheeks.

And in her body another sensation flared.

Suddenly she was as impatient as Markos for the journey to end.

Vanessa stirred, luxuriating in the softness of the deep feather mattress and the heavy warmth of the billowing duvet smothering her. In front of her, Markos was getting dressed. She sat herself up, propping up the thick pillows, pushing back her tumbled hair. As she moved, the duvet slipped a little, exposing one breast. Automatically, she covered it again.

'Just as well,' Markos told her, the grey eyes glinting briefly in appreciation as he slipped gold cufflinks through his cuffs. 'Much as I want to, there's no time for playing today.'

'Are we going back to London?' Vanessa asked sleepily. The house party at the *schloss* was over, the guests had dispersed, and their host, Leo, was off as well. Apparently his charms had won over the reluctant Anna after all, for he was leaving, so Markos said, with her in tow. Vanessa wished her well. She wished the whole world well. That was what loving Markos did to her—filled her with a joy and generosity of spirit that spilled out to everyone.

How could I have imagined living without Markos?

The very idea seemed unbelievable, unbearable. To think that she had gone to Paris with no more expectation than to see the most magical city in Europe—and had had her life transformed! Her original intention had been to spend a week in Paris and then return home to put the last of her affairs in order so that she could fulfil her even more ambitious dream of travelling around Europe—even beyond, perhaps—lashing out with a proportion of the money from the sale of her grandparents' large house, the balance safely invested, together with the money her grandparents had left her, her nest egg for the future.

Now all that seemed a universe away. All that existed to her now was Markos. Markos, Markos, Markos. His name ran like a litany in her head.

Where he would go, she would follow. To the ends of the earth if he would let her.

She felt her heart turn over. She did not know what the future would bring—could not even bring herself to think of it. She lived only in the ever-present present, the wonderful, magical *now* of being with Markos. He wanted her—and that was enough.

More, more than enough! Heaven, bliss and wonderland all combined. She gazed at him, lovelight blinding in her eyes.

He was just so incredible to look at! Even now—getting dressed, standing there in the lamplight and glowing firelight of the still-dark winter morning, lean and tall, buttoning the shirt that hid his smooth, powerful torso from her sight, reaching for the tie that was draped over the back of a chair, knotting it with skilled, casual fingers—he made her breath catch, her heart beat faster.

'London for you, yes,' he answered her. 'But I—' he made a face '—have to go to Athens. I'm sorry, but I can't get out of it.'

Her face fell. She couldn't help it.

She wanted to ask him—beg him—to let her come with him, but she knew she mustn't. If Markos had to go to Athens on business he would have no time for her, and she would not importune him. She would wait, patiently, in his vast, opulent London apartment—one of the half-dozen or so he owned in the major cities of Europe and North America—counting the hours until he returned.

'Of course,' she said bravely. 'How—how long will you be in Athens, do you think?'

She hoped she didn't sound nagging. No man liked being nagged. Especially not a man like Markos Makarios.

He gave a shrug, tightening the knot on his tie and reaching for his jacket.

'A few days—maybe a week. I don't know.'

She nodded.

'Well, I hope it all goes well—whatever the business is.'

It was Markos's turn to nod, but briefly. It wasn't business calling him to Athens; he wished it was. Anything would be preferable to the real reason. It was his father, summoning him again. He had missed out on Christmas and the New Year, spending the holiday season in Mauritius with Vanessa, a far more enjoyable experience than seeing his carping father. Of course his father had found out—nothing he did was secret from the old man, he knew that—but the berating would come in person, not over the phone. Hence the summons now.

He knew exactly how it would go. His father was old. His only son, Markos, was feckless, unfilial, self-indulgent, thinking nothing of his obligations to the Makarios name, the future of the Makarios fortunes. Had his father not suffered enough grief through Markos's mother? Did his father not deserve to have his worries and anxieties for his closing years allayed? Did his father not deserve to have his grandchildren finally around him, after so long and stubborn a prevarication by his son? And did his stubborn, disloyal son not know that he must, *must* take himself a wife to provide those essential grandchildren? A good wife, a loyal wife, a *Greek* wife, who would be faithful and true, not faithless and false. A wife who knew her duty—to give her husband sons, her father-in-law the grandchildren he deserved.

But, no, Markos was selfish and self-indulgent. He wasted his loins on harlots and whores, like the one he had spent Christmas with, fornicating in the tropics instead of coming home to take a wife for himself, a good Greek girl, any one of the dozen his father had picked out for him as worthy to bear his grandchildren…

Markos slammed down a steel door on the endlessly complaining voice echoing in his brain. *Thee mou,* but he did not want to go to Athens! Did not want to stand, teeth gritted, while his father wailed and lamented over him, accusing him of fornication and harlotry. But it had to be done—like penance. And when it was done he could escape again, get back to the life he had built for himself—a life where beautiful women like the one there in his bed now gave him everything he wanted. Everything he needed.

And who would never in a million years think about marriage.

Or children.

Or falling in love.

CHAPTER FOUR

VANESSA GAZED OUT over the night. Twenty storeys below, the River Thames gleamed, dark and opaque. She shivered. It was not just the winter's bleakness—raw and biting in the damp British air—that made her do so. The bleakness was inside her as well.

It was because Markos was not there with her.

He had been gone longer than she'd thought he would be—well over a week now. And she had counted every day, felt each one like a hard, heavy weight dragging at her.

She was missing him badly. There was an emptiness inside her, a dull, raw, sick longing like acid in her stomach, a restlessness that made her pace, now, despite the cold and the late hour, up and down on the roof terrace of his Chelsea penthouse overlooking the river. But the central-heated warmth of the luxurious interior had suddenly seemed too hot, too breathless, exacerbating the sick feeling in her stomach that had been there since she'd come back from Austria, parted from Markos.

She halted, hugging her arms around her body. *Oh, Markos, why are you away so long? I hate it when you are away from me! Please come back—please come back soon! Tomorrow—please. I miss you so much!*

The words tumbled through her head, aching and hurting.

She had it bad, she knew. Loving and wanting like this, pining when he was not there, unable to settle to anything, unable to do anything—unable to live. Just—waiting. That was all she was doing. Waiting for him to come back to her.

She couldn't even phone him or communicate with him. The mobile he had given her was for receiving his calls, not making her own to him—she didn't even know his personal number, which came up as 'private' on her screen, and phoning his PA would have been too mortifying. And, anyway, how could she phone him when he was in Athens on business? If he'd wanted to speak to her he would have done so. But he hadn't. She hadn't heard from him since she'd arrived in London.

The days had passed with brutal slowness. The Chelsea apartment was huge and luxurious, with a vast plasma-screen television, every form of sound equipment and a huge library of recordings. If she'd wanted, Housekeeping would have sent a chef up every night to cook a gourmet meal for her. But she had no interest in that. Going out shopping gave her something to do in the daytime. So did museums and concerts and the cinema and theatre matinees. She'd been to the cinema tonight to see a film, but it had been a sad love story and it had only depressed her. Besides, most of the people at the cinema had been either couples or groups of friends. She knew no one in London.

Oh, she'd met some of Markos's acquaintances when she was out and about with him, but she was hardly on their social circuit. None of them would think to invite her on her own, without Markos. Not that she would have wanted to go. The circles Markos moved in were a million miles from those she was used to, and even after five months she did not feel comfortable among such people. Only when Markos was with her could she relax, devote herself to him and pay very little attention to anyone else beyond smiling and saying whatever was required socially—which, she knew, was very little. They saw her as the woman on Markos Makarios's arm, that was all.

She didn't care. All she wanted to be, in the entire world, was the woman on Markos Makarios's arm.

She went on staring down at the cold, dark river, so far below. Waiting for Markos to come back.

So she could start living again.

Markos's mood was foul. The flight had been delayed, making him late at Heathrow, and the ten days he'd spent in Athens had been purgatory. Every last complaint he'd known his father was going to throw at him he had—and more. Worse, the old man had upped the ante disastrously by holding a dinner party to which he had invited the latest prospective 'good Greek wife' for his errant son.

Apollonia Dimistris was, Markos had instantly seen, exactly the type his father would like for him. Expensively dressed without the slightest attempt to make her attractive, she was demure to the point of inarticulate. Her mother had been more than happy to fill the conversational gaps, and Markos had been forced to behave with rigid politeness the whole evening, raining down silent curses on his father's head—most particularly when his father had made excruciatingly heavy-handed remarks about his age, decrepitude and his longing for the next Makarios generation to arrive, at which Constantia, Apollonia's mother, had smiled with an infuriatingly satisfied look on her face.

Markos had finished the evening when, finally, the dinner party had dispersed, by escaping to his own rooms in the opulent Makarios mansion and drinking too many glasses of ouzo.

For the first time in ten days his mood lifted a thread.

Thank God he was away from Athens. Thank God he was away from his father. And thank God the woman waiting for him in his London apartment was as different from Apollonia Dimistris as a succulent peach from an unripe damson!

Vanessa would be waiting for him, he knew—waiting with open arms and a warm, willing body. Beautiful and giving and oh, so eager for everything he was going to give her.

He felt himself stir as he pictured the woman who had proved such an effective means of banishing the *ennui* that had been haunting him in Paris. He'd been without sex for ten days—and that was ten days too many.

He leaned back in his soft leather seat as the car creamed down the M4 into London. Relaxing his leg muscles, he started to loosen his tie.

He wanted no delays when he got to his apartment.

'Markos!'

Vanessa's voice was faint with disbelief. For one endless moment she just stood, out on the terrace, staring at the silhouette outlined against the sliding glass doors.

'Oh, *Markos!*'

She ran to him, clinging to him, joy surging through her. His body was strong and hard against her as she wrapped herself to him, hugging him tightly, burying her face in his shoulder.

His hands slid along her cheeks and tilted her face up to look at him.

'Miss me?' he asked softly.

Anguish flared in her eyes. 'It's been *awful* without you!'

He gave a low laugh, pleased with her answer. He closed her against him more tightly yet, and she felt, with a sudden spur of both shock and excitement, that he was fully aroused.

His mouth came down on hers. Hungry, sensual, demanding. She opened to him instantly, letting his tongue forge inside, his kiss deepen, his fingers spearing into her hair. Excitement leapt in her again, raw and primitive.

For ten long, agonising days she had been without him, and

now, out of the blue, he had walked in from the bleak winter's night and turned it instantly into pulsing heat.

'*Thee mou,* but I want you!'

His voice was husky, and it sent a million shivers through her. Her breasts pressed against his hard body, their ripened peaks straining beneath the fine wool of her sweater. His hand slid from her hair, curving luxuriatingly down the length of her back to fasten over her rounded bottom, moulding her into him so that she could feel the full strength of just how much he wanted her.

He was guiding her towards the bedroom, his mouth still devouring hers, and excitement was splintering through her.

She felt herself tumble down on the bed, his weight coming on top of her. Clothes were shed—she didn't know how, didn't care, only felt the rabid, greedy hunger for him coursing through her, unstoppably. He was pressing her down, his bare, hair-roughened thigh parting hers, his hips positioning himself over her, one hand closing over hers and lifting them high over her head, so that she was splayed out for him while the other hand palmed her straining breast. His eyes were pinpoints of hunger.

She felt her back arch, her hips pressing against him, feeling the full, delicious length of him. In one swift, decisive movement he lifted away from her, then, with a slicing action, he plunged into her, right to the hilt.

She cried out, spine arching even more, arms straining where he pressed down upon her hands, and he filled her.

He sliced again, and again, and each time she cried out, more, and more breathlessly, the raw, greedy sensation of what he was making her feel buckling through her, shock after shock.

Excitement surged, and surged again, driving through her, unstoppable, feeding on itself, thrust after thrust, as every nerve and cell in her body started to fire.

'Oh, God, Markos—*Markos!*'

Sensation exploded through her. Buckling her body, sheeting through her flesh. It was unbearable. It was incredible. It was—Markos.

He came the moment she did, as if he had only been waiting for her to ignite before he gave free rein to his own demands. His body convulsed into hers, surging in its explosive release.

For one long, endless moment they writhed in unison, their bodies in tumult.

Then, with slow, absolute exhaustion, he lowered himself down on her, his body slick with sweat. His hold on her hands slackened and she felt his weight press her down.

Exhaustion drained through her. She felt as if she had run a mile at a sprint, her whole body trembling and sweating. Her mind was blown, and she was incapable of doing anything but simply lying there, eyes closed, as her breathing slowly became less ragged. Against her breasts she could feel his chest rising and falling in panting breaths.

She felt his mouth on hers, moving with dying possession.

'Now, *that*,' he said, his voice rough with repletion, 'was worth coming back for.'

His mouth slid from her, his head nestling into the pillow. She felt his dead weight over her, felt his breathing slow, his hold on her slacken. His breathing deepened, his body cooling.

He slept.

Beneath him, Vanessa lay, limbs inert and splayed, hands around Markos's smooth back. Heaviness filled her, and repletion, and a deep, deep flood of gratitude.

Markos stood under the shower, needles of water pounding over his skin. He felt fantastic. The sex had completely restored his good mood, and it had been fantastic. He tried to think of a woman he'd enjoyed more, and failed. He put the search aside. Who cared whether previous women had been as good? The one he had now was exactly what he wanted— and exactly what he had.

On top of being such a knockout, such a novelty to teach the art of pleasure to, and so openly adoring of him, she was the easiest mistress he'd ever had. She made no demands on him. She didn't ask for clothes, jewels, gifts. She didn't drop subtle-as-lead hints, didn't pester him, didn't phone him, didn't ask him where he was going or what he was doing. As for other men—well, they simply didn't exist. He could see that, and it pleased him considerably. Even Leo, whose allure for women was infamous, had no appeal for her. He'd asked her outright once whether she didn't consider his older cousin had sex appeal, and Vanessa had just looked at him as if he was mad.

His eyes shadowed briefly. An exchange he'd had with Leo at his ostentatious Schloss Edelstein fleeted back in his memory.

'Watch yourself, little cousin,' Leo had murmured caustically. 'A devoted woman can be most dangerous of all—even to someone as paranoid about marriage as you! You'd do better sticking with the ones who are open about wanting your money—you know where you are with them.'

As he'd spoken, a harsh, black light had darkened Leo's eyes. Markos had ignored it—and the warning he'd just received. So Vanessa was devoted to him? Where was the danger in that? Her very devotion made her the easiest mistress he'd ever had. Vanessa did everything he wanted, in bed and out of it, and never complained, never hinted or whinged, or played sulky or made up to other males.

Least of all did she try to manipulate him. In that she was a balm to his bruised skin after ten days of having his be-nighted father going on at him, trying to play on his son's non-existent sense of guilt for failing to produce heirs.

Hell, the last thing he wanted was offspring! Didn't he know, first hand, what it was like growing up with no reason

for his existence other than to be a bargaining chip for his mer-
cenary mother and a walking reproduction of Makarios DNA
for his father?

No, he wasn't going to think about that. Nor about his
father's exasperating but pointless machinations. He had successfully compartmentalised his life years ago. There was his
real life—running his share of the Makarios Corporation and
enjoying the plentiful fruits that that brought him, from fast
cars to beautiful women. And even when that had threatened
to become boring through familiarity and repetition the arrival
of the devoted Vanessa in his life had banished that danger.

And then there was the life he had turned away from,
where he was supposed to do his family duty and keep his
father happy. Well, his father hadn't worried much about *his*
happiness while he was growing up, so why should he worry
about his father's now?

Markos's expression hardened. After the bitter wrangling
over custody, when his father had finally got back his nine-
year-old son, had he wanted him enough to keep him at his
side? In his house? No, he'd packed him off to a private international boarding school in Switzerland, with no one
except his cousin Leo to look out for him. As for his mother,
once she'd lost the custody battle she'd had no more interest
in the child who had been merely a pawn in her financial manoeuvrings against her ex-husband. Instead she'd devoted
herself to making the most of her massive alimony by
enjoying every fleshpot she could flash herself around in.

Markos reached to snap off the shower, deliberately
turning off memory along with the water.

Stepping out, he lifted up a fresh towel and patted himself
dry, dropping it to the floor to take another larger one to wrap
around his hips. He went out into the bedroom.

The bed was empty. He frowned slightly. Vanessa had
been asleep when he'd woken, and because today he needed

to go into his London office to catch up on his business affairs he'd had no reason to wake her.

Was she making him breakfast?

She liked to do that. Another sign of her devotion, he supposed. She seemed to get a kick out of cooking for him, instead of summoning Housekeeping or having breakfast delivered from the central kitchens which serviced all the apartments.

But there was no sign of her in the huge, gleaming kitchen, glistening with polished steel surfaces. Annoyed now, Markos padded into the lounge. Also deserted. Then an idea struck him. Even after five months of intimacy Vanessa was still reluctant to come into the *en suite* bathroom if he was showering, so she often slipped into one of the *en suites* in the other bedrooms.

He went exploring, and ran her to earth.

She was in one of the bathrooms all right.

And she was throwing up.

Markos froze. His initial impulse was to retreat hurriedly, partly out of male reluctance to be in the vicinity of such an event, and partly out of consideration that the last thing she would appreciate was a witness.

Then, hard on the heels of both impulses, another thought struck him.

What the hell was she throwing up for?

Cold snaked through him. Even he, with his limited knowledge of the female reproduction system, knew about morning sickness.

No. It couldn't be. It just couldn't.

Could it?

Urgently he forced his brain to work. A stab of relief went through him. She'd been due a period just when she'd left for Austria—he remembered he'd been relieved that it would not inconvenience him, as he had missed the first few days of the fashion shoot because of a trip to New York.

Silently, on bare feet, he retreated. Vanessa, with all her

innate reserve, would not appreciate his presence right now.
Instead, he'd go and make her some coffee. She'd appreciate
that far more. Feeling virtuous, he headed away.

Shakily, Vanessa finished rinsing out her mouth, giving the
loo one last flush and an extra helping of disinfectant.

Where on earth had that come from? She'd slipped out of
bed, heading for this bathroom, and suddenly, in the doorway,
nausea had rushed up and taken her over.

With trembling fingers she pushed her tumbled hair back
and stared at her reflection. She looked as white as a ghost,
despite the fine sheen of gold dust that was the sole effect of
her freckles on her complexion.

I've just been sick in the morning.

The words tolled through her brain, but she could not
believe them. Nor their import.

I can't be pregnant—I just can't.

For a moment she just stared, thinking the unthinkable.
Then, with a wash of relief, she realised it was all right. No,
of course she couldn't be pregnant—she'd had a period in
Austria. It had been a bit of an odd period—different,
scantier—but she remembered reading somewhere that
altitude could affect menstrual cycles, and had put it down to
that.

It must be a bug, then, making her throw up. Or a last bite
from the one that she'd suffered just after Christmas, when
Markos had insisted she get antibiotics.

Maybe, she thought with a wry smile as she made her way
shakily out of the bathroom, it had been more than missing
Markos that had made her feel so rotten these past ten days.
Maybe she'd been coming down with a bug as well. The
smile faded. She didn't want to be ill with Markos—not
again—it would be such a drag for him. He hated illness, she
knew, and was highly impatient of it in himself and others.

Though he would, of course, not be horrible to her, he would hardly be glad if she were *hors de combat* so soon after that post-Christmas bug.

Well, she would just not succumb, that was all. She felt much better now, anyway. Probably throwing up had got the germs out of her and done her good.

Tightening the belt of her dressing robe resolutely, she went in search of Markos.

He was in the kitchen, putting coffee beans into the grinder.

'I'll do that!' she said instantly. She knew he hated fiddling about with the kitchen gadgets.

He turned and made space for her.

'How are you?' he asked, his dark grey eyes searching over her rapidly.

Don't let him know you're coming down with a bug, she thought. *He's only just got back; he won't want news like that.*

'Fine,' she said brightly. Then, her smile deepening into radiance, she gazed at him. 'Oh, Markos, I'm so glad you're home again! I missed you so much!'

For just the most fleeting second she thought she saw reserve in his eyes. Then it had gone. With a fond, careless flick of his finger he touched her cheek as she gazed up at him.

'Yes, you showed me last night,' he said indulgently, and watched the colour steal across her cheeks.

She was very pale, he found himself thinking. Paler than usual. Why had she not mentioned having been sick? He gave a mental shrug. The English side of him knew why—not making a fuss over things like that was a national characteristic. And if he mentioned it now she'd just be embarrassed by it.

His eyes glanced at the kitchen clock and he muttered an oath in Greek. He was running late. He had a meeting with his finance director in fifty minutes. True, the man would wait, but it was bad practice to run late in front of subordinates. It encouraged them to think they could be sloppy.

'No coffee—I'll catch breakfast in my office,' he said briskly. As he headed out of the kitchen back to the bedroom to get dressed, he called over his shoulder. 'I'll take you out to dinner tonight. Buy a new dress to wear for me. Something sexy. On second thoughts, if it's that sexy, we'll eat in—afterwards,' he added, with a throwaway taunting laugh.

Vanessa watched him go, letting her eyes feast on the angled planes of his smooth, bare, muscled back. A wave of longing went through her. Reluctantly she turned back to the coffee grinder.

As the rich fragrance of the beans struck her, so did another wave of nausea.

She clamped her lips tight and breathed deeply through her nose. No, she would *not* be sick again. She would *not* be ill.

She'd rest in the morning, then go and do what Markos asked. Buy a new dress and make herself beautiful for him.

It was what he wanted—and doing what he wanted was all she wanted to do.

She loved him so much.

Vanessa leant forward and softly blew out the two candles on the coffee table. It was stupid to waste them when Markos was not here. She glanced at the time again. Ten o'clock.

In the dining room, the table was laid for dinner. The food had been sent up, all prepared, and now waited in the fridge, as did the champagne. Everything was ready—especially her.

As she walked, the silky folds of her new dress sussurated around her long legs. The colour was daring for her—a deep, saffron-shot vermilion that she would never normally have worn. But during the fashion shoot for Leo Makarios's jewellery the stylist had put her into a similar coloured dress that had at first horrified her and then, as she'd realised that the colouring was clever enough not to clash with her red hair but instead complemented it stunningly, amazed her.

For a moment she gazed at her reflection in the mirror on the lounge wall. She did indeed look beautiful. A slow smile lit her face. Never before in her life had she been so grateful to be beautiful—because her beauty was for the man she loved. For Markos. Without it, after all, he would not have looked twice at her—but with it, oh, with it, she could lay it at his feet as her gift to him!

After all, it was all that she *could* give to him. She had nothing else. Whereas he, with his incredible wealth, could shower largesse down upon her endlessly. And he did—far more than she was comfortable with. Far more than she wanted from him. But she never said a word of that. He would be offended—how would he not be, if she rejected his largesse? And besides, all of it was to make her more beautiful. And her beauty was for him, not her. Like this dress now, costing hundreds and hundreds of pounds, purchased from one of the dozen fashion shops where he'd set up accounts for her.

But, though he lavished his largesse on her, she was as prudent as she could be with it. She bought clothes and accessories only when it was required of the life she led with him. Only when, with the slightest frown in his eyes, he remarked that he'd seen her too many times in a particular outfit. Only then would she replenish her wardrobe, so that she always looked pleasing to his eyes.

As she would now, she was sure, in this stunning dress that moulded down her slender body and flared in soft folds around her calves.

She bit her lip. Ten o'clock. It was so late. Of course, he worked ferociously hard. Running an international conglomerate was no sinecure. He spent his life travelling the world—it was no nine to five job, more like twenty-four-seven.

Self-reproach filled her. The last thing Markos needed was criticism from her for working so hard. One of the few things she could do for him, after all, was to make the hours he did not work as easy for him as she could. How could she possibly mind sitting here, waiting for him at ten o'clock?

She would sit on the sofa, slip off her shoes, and rest a while. He was a demanding lover, thrillingly so, and sleep didn't figure a whole lot in their nights together. And she'd felt extra tired today—it must be that stupid bug getting at her. The journey into the West End on her shopping expedition had been exhausting, even by taxi—she would put her feet up now, and relax.

Markos would be home soon. He was just running late, that was all.

Markos let himself into the apartment, easing his cashmere overcoat from his shoulders and tossing it on a chair in the hallway. That damn business dinner had caught him unawares, but though he'd castigated his PA for having let him in for it, he'd had no choice but to go along. It might have been tedious, enduring a formal dinner at a City livery company, but the table he'd been on had had people on it that were useful to the Makarios Corporation. So, reluctantly but resigned, he'd changed into his tuxedo in his private apartment next to his office and been driven off by Stelios in his corporate limo. It was a bore, but it had to be done.

But now, at last, it was over, and he was home.

He walked into the lounge. The lights were set low, and the scent of fresh flowers caught at him.

So, too, did the splash of vivid, fiery colour against the white sofa. He walked forward, a smile pulling at his mouth.

Sleeping Beauty in person.

His eyes washed over Vanessa in the low light. God, but she was so lovely! For a moment he stood looking down at her as she slept, her long limbs relaxed, entwined with silk. Her breasts rose and fell, the bodice of her dress revealing their soft sweet mounds. He felt desire start in him, his blood quicken.

Time to wake Sleeping Beauty by the traditional means.
But in his case, it would go a lot further than a kiss.

He dropped down beside her and lowered his mouth to
hers. Her mouth was like velvet.

CHAPTER FIVE

CAREFULLY, VANESSA STEPPED out of the limo. Out in the chill of the still wintry night she was glad of the *faux* fur coat she was wearing over her thin evening gown. But she was only exposed to the elements for the few moments it took for Markos to unfold his long, lean form from the interior and take her arm to walk her into the famous West End hotel, the doors instantly opened for them by the attentive doorman.

She'd been to the hotel before with Markos, but tonight they were going to a private party being held in one of the function rooms. It was going to be a lavish affair; Markos had wanted her dressed to the nines, and had even come with her to choose her gown. It was a glittering gold sheath, with a décolletage lower than she was comfortable with but which didn't seem to bother Markos in the least. Indeed, his eyes had gleamed appreciatively when she'd finally emerged from the ministrations of the stylist, hairdresser and manicurist who had been at work on her for two hours that evening.

'You look breathtaking!' he'd told her. 'It only needs one more item…'

As Vanessa progressed across the foyer of the hotel she could feel the 'item' nestling in the valley of her enhanced cleavage—a pendant diamond that glittered like an iridescent rainbow.

'Oh, Markos,' she'd breathed, eyes wide, as he'd fastened it around her neck, 'it's *beautiful.*'

Now, as she walked beside him—the woman on Markos Makarios's arm—she knew she looked as beautiful as she ever could. Whatever that bug had been that had been pulling her down, she seemed to have shaken it off at last. She felt healthy again—wonderful, in fact—and it was reflected in the mirror. There was a glow in her complexion, a brightness in her eyes, that was enhancing her beauty. And it was all for Markos. She felt her heart squeeze with emotion as she tilted her head to gaze up at him.

It overwhelmed her sometimes, the strength of her feelings, overpowering her. He was just so handsome, so wonderful, so devastating, so gorgeous. She could gaze at him all day, every day, every night, for ever and ever…

'Markos!'

A voice called out from a little way away. A man was walking towards them, clad in a tuxedo like Markos, and speaking in Greek to him. At her side, Vanessa could feel Markos tense slightly as he paused.

'Cosmo,' he acknowledged.

The other man walked up to them. He was about Markos's age, but nowhere near as good-looking, with swarthy features and a soft jawline.

More Greek was exchanged, but even as the other man was speaking to Markos his eyes were drawn to Vanessa. She didn't like it. She was used to male attention, which came in two types—the type that was appreciative but polite, and the type that made her feel uncomfortable. This was definitely the latter. Instinctively, she felt herself stiffen.

'Come, Markos, don't be selfish—introduce me!' The other man had suddenly swapped to English, and now his black eyes were openly lapping her up.

Did Markos hesistate? Vanessa was sure he did, and she

was grateful. Then the other man said something else in Greek and gave a laugh.

'Vanessa, this is Cosmo Dimistris. Cosmo—'

But Cosmo had not waited for the completion of the formal introduction. He helped himself to one of Vanessa's hands, enclosing it between his own. They felt large and beefy.

'Hot, Markos, definitely hot—you certainly know how to pick them!'

Even though he was speaking to Markos, his eyes were still greedily on Vanessa.

With a jerk she pulled her hand free. Cosmo was saying something else to Markos, with another laugh. Whatever it was he said, it did not go down well with Markos. Not that Cosmo seemed deterred—rather the opposite. Swapping to English he went on, 'Come and have a drink—there's plenty of time.'

'Not for us, thanks,' Markos replied evenly. He nodded curtly at Cosmo and set off with Vanessa towards the bank of elevators at the far side of the lobby. She was glad. Cosmo Dimistris, whoever he was, was a creep.

'Who was that?' Vanessa found herself asking. She hoped he was someone they wouldn't run into again.

'No one you need bother about,' Markos answered tightly. He hadn't expected to see Cosmo Dimistris here, and he hadn't liked the way he had been so obviously taken with Vanessa. Not that Vanessa had seemed the slightest bit taken in return—but then she made it abundantly clear that no other male existed apart from him. His eyes glanced down at her. *Theos,* she really was stunning! Always beautiful, tonight she had surpassed herself, looking so breathlessly alluring that he was not surprised Cosmo had slavered over her. There was a radiance about her that was almost incandescent.

The bank of elevators was in front of him and he halted, reaching to jab at the control button. Almost simultaneously one set of doors sliced open and two women emerged. One middle-aged, one very young.

Markos froze.

Hell! Why in God's name had that cretin Cosmo not thought to warn him?

The answer came with a savage lack of humour.

Probably he thought it would be amusing.

Well, it wasn't amusing. Not in the slightest.

In the event, it only lasted the briefest moment. Constantia Dimistris took in the situation instantly. Markos could see that she'd recognised him—how could she not have?—but there was barely a split second between her recognition, of him and who he was with, and her sailing forward without acknowledging him.

Her daughter, however, was less worldly-wise. Markos saw Apollonia hesitate, her eyes flying to him. To his intense irritation, a blush started to flush through her face as she stopped dead in front of him.

'Apollonia!'

Her mother's voice was sharp, commanding, and her eyes darted compellingly at her daughter. For a second Apollonia looked bewildered, as though she could not understand why her mother was not acknowledging the presence of the man she hoped would become her future son-in-law. Then, excruciatingly slowly, her eyes flickered to the woman beside Markos Makarios.

Instantly the blush deepened and a soft noise escaped her throat, mingled shock and, Markos could see, fascination. He was not surprised—doubtless Constantia Dimistris would have instructed her virginal daughter that 'men were different', but her carefully sheltered existence would have ensured that Apollonia would never have seen in the flesh visible proof of that 'difference'. The most she'd have seen would have been photos in celebrity magazines of fashionable nightspots with coy captions like *Greek magnate, Markos Makarios, and friend.*

To his intense relief, Constantia summoned her daughter again, even more sharply, and this time she responded. Still blushing, she hurried after her mother. With grim smoothness Markos ushered Vanessa inside the elevator, jabbed the button, and the doors slid shut.

Hell, thought Markos, he could have done without that. He really could have done without it! Typical of Cosmo Dimistris to think it amusing not to warn him that his mother and sister were staying at the hotel—Markos hadn't even known they were in London.

His expression tightened. Had Constantia Dimistris deliberately trailed her daughter to London because his father had told her his son was still there? Well, if so, maybe that unfortunate encounter just now had served a useful purpose. He'd better make sure he took Vanessa with him wherever he went until the Dimistris females had taken themselves off again! Nothing like having your mistress in evidence to keep unwanted would-be brides out of your hair...

His eyes flickered to Vanessa again, taking in her rich, glittering beauty. What man in their right mind would want a wife when he had so beautiful a creature devoted to him? Deliberately, he let his finger trail along the low-cut line of her bodice, and saw her respond to his touch, just as he had known she would.

He gave a low laugh, good mood restored.

It was, indeed, a lavish affair. The huge, opulently decorated suite was thronged with people, and she could hear a polyglot buzz of languages. Vanessa didn't have any idea who was actually hosting the affair, or what it was for, but it didn't bother her. She was simply at Markos's side, and that was that. He could converse in at least four languages, and she only in

English, so a lot of the time she was simply smiling and sipping her glass of champagne. Even when the conversation was in English she said very little. Not that many people spoke directly to her, anyway, and then it was usually men. If they were the type like Cosmo Dimistris she was glad when they didn't.

He was here; she'd seen him on the far side of the room, when the throng had parted a moment. He'd been laughing, showing a lot of teeth, and instinctively Vanessa had turned slightly away. Presumably he was one of the many guests here, but he hadn't come up to Markos again and she was glad of it. Instead, since Markos was talking in French to a middle-aged man, she went back to doing what she instinctively did whenever his attention was elsewhere— looking at him.

She loved looking at him, taking in everything about him, from the arch of his eyebrows to the lines indenting around his mouth when he laughed, from the way his dark hair was oh-so-slightly ruffled to the way his dinner jacket sat taut across his shoulders. Every detail of his endless physical perfection. She could just gaze and gaze, and let her heart fill up with emotion and flow over the brim...

'Vanessa?'

The voice was amused, indulgent, and she blinked. Markos had stopped speaking French and was glancing down at her.

'Excuse me for a moment, will you?'

She nodded at once. 'Of course,' she murmured. Markos smiled briefly at her and made off with the other man, joining a couple some way off—another middle-aged man and a richly dressed elderly woman with a grand air about her. Other people moved, and she could no longer see Markos. For a moment Vanessa just stood there, feeling stupidly bereft.

Then a voice spoke beside her.

'Alas, you've been abandoned. How foolish of Markos.'

Her head twisted just as her heart sank. The florid features of Cosmo Dimistris loomed at her side.

Automatically she lifted her champagne glass. It was both a psychological and a physical barrier. She took a sip, uncomfortably aware of the other man's perusal.

'Yes,' mused Cosmo, his eyes fixed on her, 'Markos certainly knows how to pick the most luscious fruit on the tree. Have you been with him long?'

Vanessa's smile was tight, nothing more than social civility required.

'We met in September.'

Cosmo's heavy eyebrows rose. 'You've lasted well,' he remarked, his Greek accent pronounced. 'But then, you are exceptional.' He leaned towards her. 'And only the best will do for Markos Makarios, of course.' He gave a laugh that Vanessa did not like. Automatically her eyes went searching past Cosmo's shoulders to where Markos was still engaged with the French group. Almost she started forward, to go towards him, then stopped herself. He must be talking business, and if he'd wanted her beside him he'd have taken her over.

So she held her ground. If she said as little as possible to this unappealing acquaintance of Markos, he might take the hint and move on.

But it seemed Cosmo Dimistris had no inclination to move on. He took a mouthful of whatever he was drinking, which looked like some kind of highball.

'So,' he said, his eyes still fixed on her, 'you're making the most of him, I take it?' Casually he reached out and touched the diamond pendant with the tip of a fat finger. 'Very pretty.' As he took his finger away it seemed to slip suddenly, and touch her bare skin. It took all her poise not to flinch. 'I'd give you emeralds, myself. Far more dramatic for your colouring. Tell me, what are your plans for the future? I would be interested in knowing.' He paused. 'Very interested.' Again the hot eyes worked over her, in a way she hated.

Repulsion warred with sheer disbelief. Some man she had been reluctantly introduced to a bare hour or so ago was asking her about her plans for the future? Vanessa could only stare blankly, not knowing how to deal with such an intrusive question.

Oblivious, Cosmo Dimistris took another mouthful of his highball.

'It would be quite funny, really,' he went on. 'Keeping it in the family, so to speak—I would be happy—more than happy—' he bestowed another louche look at her '—to provide a convenient solution to your predicament.'

Vanessa was baffled. What on earth was he on about? She neither knew nor cared. She just wanted him to go away and Markos to return to her side.

She stiffened as Cosmo Dimistris leant forward suddenly, moving deliberately into her body space.

'How loath Markos will be,' he breathed, 'to relinquish so delectable a mistress as you—but his loss would be my gain, no? And yours too, of course. I would be as generous as he, I assure you—you would not lose by coming to me.' The hot eyes were all over her again, speculative, lascivious.

Vanessa jerked back, the movement sharp and instinctive.

'Excuse me.' Her voice was clipped. Shock and disbelief mingled in her. This repulsive man had actually *said* that to her? She turned away, lurching forward towards where Markos was still talking to the French group. She could not stay where she was and let that disgusting man talk to her in such a way. A shudder went through her, as if something unclean had touched her skin.

'Markos—' Her voice was pitched with relief as she reached him, her hand automatically going around his forearm as if he were a life-raft.

The Frenchman who'd been talking fell silent. Realising she must have interrupted him with her exclamation, she gave a shaky smile. 'Please—do excuse me,' she murmured a little breathlessly. She gave a social smile, her fingers closing around Markos's arm a little tighter.

The Frenchman did not resume talking. Nor did anyone else say anything. There was a sudden silence. Then, abruptly, the elderly woman and the other man moved away. At her side, Vanessa suddenly realised that Markos was tense. As the couple moved away the man who'd been speaking said something again, in rapid French. Markos nodded curtly, then turned away, drawing Vanessa with him.

'I'm ... I'm sorry,' she stammered. 'I didn't mean to interrupt. It's just that—'

'I told you I would only be a few minutes.' Markos's voice sounded sharp.

Vanessa stared, a hollow feeling in her throat.

'What—what is it?'

She saw his lips press together, and then he spoke.

'That was the Duchesse de Nerailles-Courcy,' he said tightly.

Vanessa blinked. 'I'm sorry, I don't know who she is.'

'Well, obviously not.' Markos sounded impatient, then gave a sharp sigh. 'Look, forget it—all right? It's too late now. But, please, next time I ask you to wait for me, I'd appreciate it if you did so.'

There was a sharpness in his voice that Vanessa had never heard before. Slowly, without realising she was doing it, she let her hand fall from his arm.

'I'm sorry, Markos,' she said. Her throat was constricted.

He gave another sigh, more heavy this time.

'Vanessa—some people have a very relaxed attitude, and some, like the Duchesse, do not. She just isn't someone I could introduce you to.'

'Too grand, huh?' Vanessa tried to put a laugh into her

voice, though it still sounded shaky. But then, she felt pretty shaky herself, with Markos's unexpected sharpness coming right after that horrible friend of his speaking to her like that. 'Doesn't she speak to bourgeois commoners like me?' She forced herself to sound light-hearted, self-deprecating.

Markos's expression was odd. Probably, she thought, because she'd hit the nail on the head, and he was embarrassed by having to admit to the Frenchwoman's snobbery.

Then someone a little way away was hailing him, and the moment passed as he responded and led Vanessa across, his hand cupping around her elbow.

'Guido—it's good to see you.' He launched into fluent Italian.

Gratefully, Vanessa resumed her safe and familiar role—the woman at Markos Makarios's side. Deliberately, she put aside the two upsetting incidents that had just happened. They meant nothing. She mustn't think about them. She was with Markos.

That was all that counted.

The remainder of the evening passed without further incident, and gradually Vanessa's spirits were restored. OK, so she didn't belong in this glittering, high society world that the man she loved lived in, but that didn't mean she couldn't learn to belong. Unpleasant incidents like those that had happened earlier were rare—in fact, she didn't think they'd ever really happened before. True, she'd been on the receiving end of some dagger-drawn looks, but they had invariably been from other women, and it had not taken her long to twig that the cause of their unfriendliness was that *she* was the one with Markos Makarios. Women were all over him like flies to a honeypot, and she could hardly be surprised at that when she was so smitten with him! She was bound to encounter jealousy and resentment from other women less fortunate than herself. Markos himself never gave her cause for anxiety in that respect. He was obviously accustomed to being fêted by females, but he never flirted with any of them—never made her think he was more interested in them than he was in her. He was always attentive, always possessive. It was a warm feeling that set a golden glow around her heart.

As they moved around, clearly a couple, smiling and sipping champagne, or nibbling the delicious canapés that circulated endlessly, a stray phrase came back to her. She tried to banish it, because it had come from that odious man who had said such creepy stuff to her, but for all that it repeated itself in her mind.

Future plans, the man had said. What were her future plans?

A faint furrow creased between her eyebrows. She pushed the thought away. She didn't want to think about things like that. After all, she had no plans. She was simply with Markos, that was all.

For how long?

The words pricked into her consciousness like an insect bite. She brushed them aside as if they were just that. She wouldn't think about things like the future, or how long she had with Markos. If she didn't think about them, they didn't exist. She was too happy, too blissful, too floating on her wonderful, unbelievable personal cloud nine to think about anything like that! Markos was so good to her, so wonderful. It was enough—of course it was enough!—just to have what she had.

And she had so much. She had everything her heart could desire—the most wonderful man in the world to love, who wanted her with him.

Her eyes went to him, standing so tall, so devastatingly gorgeous beside her. Her heart swelled with love.

As she gazed, happy to do nothing more than that, to take in the perfection of his profile, he seemed to sense it, pausing minutely in his conversation. His eye caught hers, and for a brief, shivering moment he just looked at her. She could read the message in them as clearly as if he'd spoken aloud. Then his long dark lashes swept down and he went on talking again.

But at her back she could feel the pressure of his fingers, softly smoothing the satin of her gown, conveying their unmistakable message and making her limbs feel weak.

They left very soon after.

Vanessa slid the ice-blue cocktail dress over her head and felt it slither down her body. Brushing her hair aside, she crooked her arms back to zip it up, then stared at her reflection in the huge mirror in the dressing room off Markos's bedroom.

She frowned. Had she put on weight? The material seemed to be clinging slightly around her stomach and hips. The last time she'd worn this particular dress a few weeks ago it had fitted perfectly. She breathed in, and looked at her reflection again. She *looked* all right, it was just that the dress *felt* a tad more clingy than it had done before. Maybe she was imagining things. Maybe it had shrunk slightly with cleaning.

Surely she couldn't have put on weight. She was scrupulous about what she ate. Naturally slim, now that she was with Markos she knew she could not afford to lose her figure even minutely. She wanted to look perfect for him the whole time. The trouble was, all this high life seemed to come accompanied by the most gorgeous gourmet food wherever they went, even when they ate in, and it was all so tempting! That was one reason why she was such a regular habituée of the gym and pool in the basement of the apartment block, or of the fitness suites in the hotels they stayed at when they were abroad. Exercise toned her body, and kept her in peak condition for Markos.

It also helped to pass the time when he was working.

She frowned again, breathing out slowly. Yes, the material was definitely brushing against her stomach and hips. She bit her lip. She would have to cut back on the food and increase her workout time, that was all. It might only be a few pounds she'd put on, but there was, she could see now, a discernible swell to her tummy that she was sure had not been there before.

Maybe it was just monthly bloating, of course. Not that she usually suffered much from PMS, but perhaps having an active sex life—a *very* active sex life, she thought with an inward blush—was making a difference of some kind. If it was PMS, though, it was a bit odd, as she'd only just finished another period. But then that had been an odd period too— just as the one before, up in the mountains, had been odd. Much shorter. Different.

Out in the bedroom, she heard the phone start to ring, distracting her thoughts as she hurried to answer it. It must be Markos, saying where to meet him that evening.

'Hello?' she said, picking the handset up, sounding very slightly breathless.

'Good evening, Vanessa. Did I disturb you in bed? Or in the bath, perhaps?'

The male voice was definitely not Markos. Nor could it possibly be either Taki or Stelios, the two Greek members of his staff who acted as a mix of bodyguards, chauffeurs and general factotums to him.

'Who is this?' she asked, more sharply than she usually spoke.

A laugh came down the line.

'Forgotten me so soon? I'll have to remind you, won't I? We met the other evening, when Markos was so foolish as to abandon you.'

Vanessa stiffened. It was that creepy friend of Markos's. Cosmo Dimistris. Well, whatever he wanted, she didn't want to speak to him.

'Markos isn't here at the moment,' she answered, making her voice impersonal and formal. 'I'll tell him you called. Do you want to leave a message?'

Damn, she was sounding like a secretary. But she just wanted Cosmo Dimistris off the line.

The laugh came again. It sounded distinctly sleazy.

'The only message I'd like to leave Markos is that you've

told me I'm better in bed than he is—but it's a little soon for that. Not too soon, I hope. Tell me, have you thought any more about moving on yet? I'm flying to Mexico next week. Come with me—I'll be throwing some wild parties. You'd be really hot—'

Vanessa dropped the phone as if it were suddenly burning. As if she had just been touched by something slimy and disgusting.

Oh, God, that horrible, horrible man! How *could* he say such creepy stuff to her? She hoped he wouldn't turn into a pest. Surely he had got the message now?

But the following afternoon she discovered that Cosmo Dimistris was about as thin-skinned as a rhinoceros. She was walking back into the lobby after having had her regular beauty treatments in Sloane Street when the concierge came round from the desk.

'Special delivery,' he said.

She took the package, wondering what it was. Up in the apartment she had her answer. It was a slim jewel case, gift-wrapped inside the courier packaging. A card was tucked into the ribbons. Staring, she read it.

The necklace that goes with this is in Mexico. Phone me and it's yours.

A telephone number was scrawled underneath. There was no name, and she didn't need one. She knew exactly the creep who'd sent this insulting and objectionable 'present'.

Tight-lipped, she opened the case, revealing a bracelet set with emeralds. Her fingers clenched. For a moment she just stared at the bracelet, wondering how on earth she was going to get rid of it. She had no idea where that odious man lived, and didn't want to. She clicked the lid shut and turned the box over. To her relief the jeweller's name was on the base. She could just have it returned to them. They would know who had bought it and get it back to him.

A footfall behind her made her jerk her head back.

Markos was walking out of his study.

Instinctively, breath catching, she whipped the case and its wrapping behind her back, a horrified expression on her face. She'd had no idea Markos was home.

'What have you got there?' He sauntered towards her.

'Nothing,' she said automatically.

He gave a slanting smile. 'You're looking very guilty over nothing.'

'It's just junk mail,' Vanessa replied quickly.

Markos's eyebrows rose.

'That gets stopped in the postroom.' A gleam entered his eye. 'Don't tell me. It's something secret. A pregnancy testing kit, perhaps, hmm?'

The gleam had become a glint, and there was something in it that disturbed Vanessa, but she was too shocked by what he'd just said to do anything other than stare open-mouthed.

'A *what?*' she echoed weakly.

Something shifted in Markos's expression at her response.

'So not the worst, then?' he responded smoothly. 'What about the next worst? Something from a secret admirer, perhaps?'

The words were humorous, and so was the tone. But to her horror Vanessa felt the blood drain from her cheeks. As it did, she saw Markos's face change. Before she could move he had come up to her and snaked his hand around her back, drawing her hand forward.

Wordlessly, without looking at her, he took the jewel case from her.

In dead silence he flicked the lid open, then glanced at the accompanying card with the message on it.

'And just *who* is inviting you to Mexico to collect the rest of these emeralds?'

Vanessa felt a wave of ice go down her spine. Never had she heard Markos speak in such tones to her—not even the other evening, when he'd been so curt about her interrupting that stuck-up Duchess. To Taki, sometimes, or Stelios, if he was out of humour or something had been fouled up, but even then she had never heard that cold steel in his voice.

She stared helplessly.

'Well?'

His face was grim and closed.

Still she could not answer, paralysed with ice in her veins. Chill grey eyes bored into her. This wasn't Markos. It couldn't be Markos...

'Do you intend to go?'

The words cut through her paralysis. Her pupils flared.

'Of course not! I wouldn't go near that disgusting man with a bargepole!'

Something changed in Markos's eyes.

'What man? Who is he? Who sent these?'

Vanessa took a step back, throwing her head up.

'That horrible man at the hotel the other day! Cosmo Dimistris, or whatever his name was!'

Markos's eyes narrowed. 'Cosmo? *Cosmo* sent you this bracelet? What the hell gave him the idea that you'd take it from him? Or go to Mexico to collect on the necklace?'

There was anger in his voice. More than anger.

Accusation.

Something snapped in Vanessa.

'Well, it wasn't me, believe me! He came up with the charming idea all on his own. He slimed up to me at the party when you were off talking to that stuck-up French duchess who cut me dead! And you can send it back to him right now, OK? Along with his oh-so-charming offer to take me on as his mistress!'

'What?' Markos's voice was a knife-cut.

Breath hissed in Vanessa's throat.

'Exactly! He had the almighty gall to stand there and tell me I could be his mistress for the asking!'

Greek spat from him. Vanessa didn't ask for a translation. It would not be fit for her ears, she knew. His expression was thunderous.

'He was lucky I didn't slap his face on the spot!' she went on, anger still burning in her. 'That's why I rushed up to you and interrupted you the way I did and upset the Duchess. I didn't mean to be bad-mannered, but that creep really upset me. Saying I could be his *mistress!*'

Markos's face was still grim, but she could see the anger was no longer directed at her, but at his horrible friend. He gave a sudden snort of grim humour.

'I trust you told him you were still mine? And that you were *not* in the market for a change of protector.'

A shudder went through her.

'Markos—don't! Not even in jest. It's just too horrible.'

His mouth pressed tightly. 'I was not jesting, believe me. Cosmo Dimistris can forget all about poaching my mistress from me!'

Vanessa's hands clenched. 'Markos—please. Don't even say that word. Not even about a creep like him.' She shuddered again. *'Mistress.'* There was revulsion in her voice.

Markos stepped forward, his hand going around the nape of her neck. He tilted her face up to him with his other hand and dropped a light kiss on her mouth.

'No man's mistress but mine,' he said reassuringly, as he let her go again.

But Vanessa was still upset, even after this comforting gesture.

'No, please—don't use that word. It's so horrible. I know you're just trying to make a joke of it, but—'

'A joke?' There was a blank note in his voice.

Vanessa gazed up at him, her expression confused. 'Well, yes, of course it's a joke…saying I'm your mistress…'

Markos dropped his hand. 'You think it a *joke* to be my mistress?' His expression was suddenly taut.

The confusion deepened in Vanessa's eyes. 'I—I don't understand.'

'What do you not understand? You've been my mistress for half a year, and in all that time you—'

She jerked back.

Staring up at him.

Disbelieving.

'Markos—don't say that. Please.' Her voice was faint suddenly.

The planes of his face were still taut, but now the expression in his eyes had changed to blankness.

'Don't say what? Vanessa, you are not making sense.'

'Mistress.' Her voice was fainter still. 'You keep saying *mistress*. It's a joke, isn't it, Markos? Just a joke. Saying that to me? Calling me that?'

Her eyes were huge in her face. In her chest, she could feel her heart rate quicken, anxiety build. Something was going wrong here—she was getting it wrong. She had to be! Markos spoke such superb English she sometimes forgot he was half-Greek. Maybe she was confusing him.

He was still gazing at her blankly.

'I repeat,' he said, and she could hear the edge underlying his words as he spelt them out. 'Why do you think being my mistress is a joke?'

Vanessa shut her eyes, then opened them. She had to explain. He'd got hold of completely the wrong end of the stick.

'No—you don't understand. I mean, I *know* you are just using the word "mistress" as a joke, but I just… I just don't see it as funny, Markos. I'm sorry. It's such a repellent thought—'

His face had stilled.

'You think it *repellent* to be my mistress?' The anger was there now, unhidden.

And suddenly, with a ghastly sick realisation, Vanessa realised that it was not Markos who did not understand her—but *she* who did not understand *him.*

Oh, God, he means it. He really means it. He's not joking, he's not making fun of the word—he means it.

She heard herself speak, still in that same faint voice.

'You mean it, don't you? When you say *mistress* you mean it.'

Angry exasperation flashed in his eyes.

'Why on earth should I *not* mean it? Of course you are my mistress! *Thee mou,* you've been living with me long enough!'

She started clutching at straws. His English was not perfect. It couldn't be. It must be that he didn't understand the implications of the word *mistress.* She was searching desperately for some comfort, some reassurance…

He took a step towards her, reaching for her.

'Vanessa, what is this? If that louse Cosmo has upset you, I'm truly sorry. He will never come near you again, I promise.' His voice was conciliatory, caressing. His eyes washed over her, warm and familiar. 'You are mine—all mine—you know you are.'

He made to embrace her, all his anger gone now completely. He was Markos again, the Markos she knew…

Or did she?

She stepped back, away from him. Her heart was still racing, eyes huge and uncertain.

'Your mistress.' There was flatness in her voice.

Fear.

Markos was just looking at her. Slowly, he nodded.

'Yes, my mistress. Vanessa, what *is* this? Why are you

being like this? What is happening?' For a moment he just went on looking at her, searching her face, a frown of incomprehension on his brow.

Vanessa could say nothing. Her throat was too tight. Then, suddenly, Markos's brows snapped together.

'My God,' he breathed abruptly, 'what else did he say to you? Cosmo Dimistris—what else did he say to you?'

There was a harsh urgency in his voice.

'N—nothing,' she made herself answer. She saw his face relax once more as he breathed out. He looked relieved. She wondered at it momentarily, then forgot it. Her heart was still racing.

There has to be a misunderstanding. He can't understand what that word means in English. He just can't!

'So why are you so upset?'

She gazed at him. This was Markos, her own Markos, the man she loved absolutely, completely. She mustn't be upset. It was just semantics, that was all—a word he didn't understand in English. It probably didn't translate properly from the Greek, that was all.

She mustn't let it get to her!

Deliberately, she took a deep breath. What did a word matter? Nothing—nothing at all compared to what she had with Markos. And that was far too precious to risk by getting stupidly upset by something as irrelevant as a single word.

'Vanessa?'

His voice had changed minutely. The slightest trace of an edge of impatience was back in it.

She swallowed. No, she wasn't going to be upset. It was stupid of her, unnecessary, idiotic. And it was all the fault of that creepy friend of his and his repulsive proposition. Markos was nothing like that! He was totally different—affectionate and considerate and caring.

No wonder she loved him as much as she did.

Her voice choked as she answered, 'I'm sorry. Oh, Markos, I'm sorry. I'm being an idiot! Making a fuss over nothing. Please forgive me.'

He opened his arms to her and she went into them, feeling them fold around her, safe and strong. The man she loved.

'Foolish girl,' he murmured, and started to kiss her. And in moments she had forgotten everything except her bliss in being in his embrace.

CHAPTER SIX

MARKOS STIRRED. He didn't want to get up, but he knew he could not go on lying here with Vanessa in his arms any longer. The only reason he was at the apartment at this hour was to say goodbye to her. He was flying this evening to Melbourne on business, but only for two days, and the trip would be so gruelling he was not going to subject Vanessa to it for such a short time. When he had to, he could do without her.

Not that he wanted to. As she lay, head on his chest, hair streaming like a red-gold banner across him, her body soft and warm and exhausted from the delights they had both just experienced, it took a real effort of will to put her aside and get up.

She looked at him hazily.

'Is it time already?' she asked. He could hear the regret in her voice.

'I won't be gone for long,' he told her reassuringly. 'I'll be back by the weekend.' He twisted round to drop a last kiss on her mouth, before heading to the bathroom to shower.

When he emerged she had got out of bed, wrapping her body in a long peach-coloured peignoir, her long hair still tousled and sexy. A pang went through him. He did not want to leave her. For a moment he was on the verge of telling her to get dressed and packed and come with him, then sense prevailed. Not only was it a gruelling flight, but he would have to spend at least one evening with his aunt, Leo's mother, who'd moved to Melbourne after she was widowed to be with relatives on her mother's side. Obviously he wouldn't be able to take Vanessa with him when he visited *her.*

On the other hand, he mused, his aunt was a bosom bow of Constantia Dimistris, even at such long distance. For his aunt to see that he had brought his mistress to Australia with him might feed back to Constantia and help convince her that he was *not* in the market for her daughter!

A familiar tide of irritation swept through him. Constantia had phoned his office twice already, once to invite him to escort her and Apollonia to the theatre, and then once again. He'd been grateful for a business dinner as an excuse. The woman was making herself far too obvious.

His frown deepened. As for Cosmo Dimistris... Cosmo had definitely overstepped the mark of what had never been more than a highly casual friendship, born of moving in the same circles in Athens and a host of internecine business connections that meshed around wealthy Greek families. Of course it was to be expected that Cosmo would lust after Vanessa—what red-blooded man wouldn't?—but to make a move on her like that was totally out of order. It wasn't just a question of trying to poach from a friend; it was that anyone who looked at Vanessa could see how devoted she was to the man she was already with, so Cosmo didn't even have the excuse that Vanessa was looking restless, as if she wanted to move on herself.

His mouth tightened, a grim look entering his eye. He knew why Cosmo was acting as if Vanessa would soon become available—it was because he was assuming that it would not be long before *he,* Markos, became unavailable! Taking a wife would mean that a mistress would have to be put aside.

In ill humour, Markos strode to his closet to yank out a shirt. Loath as he was to have to be that blunt, maybe he was just going to have to spell out to Cosmo—and Constantia Dimistris for that matter!—that there was no way he was going to marry Apollonia.

Or any woman.

And if that meant a final showdown with his father, telling him once and for all to stay out of his life, then so be it!

His eyes went to Vanessa, who was busy remaking the bed—she never seemed to leave that to the maid service, Markos noted—and his expression softened. *There* was all the woman he wanted. Adoring, sensual, undemanding—the list of reasons why Vanessa was the perfect mistress for him went on and on.

He slid his arms down the sleeves, and shrugged the shirt over his shoulders, flexing their musculature as he did so. His body had the invigorating afterglow that sex with Vanessa always gave it. His eyes worked over her slender, graceful figure as she leant over the bed to plump the pillows. She really was an absolute gem of a mistress! Definitely his best ever.

He reached for his cufflinks and started to slip them on. A frown teased along his brow.

He still didn't get why that bad scene had happened before he'd whisked her to bed. Cosmo had been way out of line sending her those emeralds, and, yes, for a moment he'd been sharp with her when he'd thought she might have been inviting Cosmo's attentions. But as soon as she'd rejected that possibility he'd made it clear to her that he wasn't blaming her in any way. Let alone, for heaven's sake, encouraging her to leave him!

The frown deepened. Why had she flipped like that when he'd reassured her that she was his mistress for the foreseeable future? It didn't make sense.

He gave a mental shrug and put the niggle aside. She was

probably hormonal right now, or whatever, making her hypersensitive. The frown flashed again momentarily. Damn. If she were hormonal now, she'd probably be *hors de combat* right about the time he came back from Melbourne.

He cast his mind back. When had she last been out of action? He tried to remember, but failed. It seemed longer ago than usual...

'Markos?'

Vanessa had finished tidying the bed and was coming up to him. His mind diverted instantly. God, she looked so good! Tall and glowing, that fantastic hair tumbling free over her shoulders, her beauty just so stunning...

'Do you want to eat before you leave?' she asked him. 'Can I make you something? Or coffee?'

For answer, he scooped her up in his arms. She was soft and pliant and warm. So good to hold. He stood for a moment, just savouring the feeling of holding her.

He didn't want to let her go.

But the flight to Melbourne would not wait, not even for first-class passengers, and he had to be on it. Reluctantly he stepped back.

'Just coffee,' he told her. Then, his hands still on her upper arms, he looked down into her eyes.

'I'm going to miss you,' he said softly.

Was there a sudden stricken look in her eyes? Something speared through him. He seriously did not want to go right now.

But business was business. He had meetings to go to, deals to set up. Only he could do that, not one of his managers. For a moment he wished the whole Makarios Corporation to perdition! He should do what Leo had just done—swan off somewhere tropical and take some R&R. With a beautiful woman to keep him company, of course, the way Leo had! So what was stopping him from doing likewise?

On impulse he spoke.

'When I get back there'll be a few things I'll need to sort here, then how would you like a holiday? Somewhere there's no winter. We could sail the yacht from its Caribbean mooring, go island-hopping and catch some rays.'

The stricken look vanished, and it was like the sun coming out in her eyes.

'That would be wonderful!' Vanessa breathed. Her arms came around him and she laid her head on his chest, hugging him tightly. 'Oh, Markos, you are so *good* to me. I do so love y—' Her voice cut off, as if she had pressed a switch, then it resumed. 'I do so love being on holiday with you. It's just the best thing ever!'

He lifted her face from his chest and cupped it in his hands.

'*You're* the best thing ever, Vanessa,' he said, and his voice was a caress.

Then, reluctantly, he put her aside, and went on getting ready to go.

'...forty-eight, forty-nine, *fifty!*' Vanessa breathed out in exhausted triumph and lay back on the exercise mat. Fifty sit-ups: she'd earned a breather. But not for too long. She was only halfway through her workout, and there were the weights machines still to do. Still, the cardiovascular session was over and she was glowing, with a light sheen of sweat over her whole body.

She limbered to her feet. If she had been putting on a few extra pounds, working out was the best way to shed them. With Markos away, exercising in the luxury gym in the apartment block basement was also a much better way to use her time than moping around like she'd done last time, when that bug had been coming on. Still, at least the bug hadn't developed as badly as the nasty one she'd got when they'd come back from Mauritius in the New Year, when she'd had to take those ghastly antibiotics. But whatever it had been, she felt fine now—totally fine. She took a deep breath, got her body into balance, and went into some floor stretches. Her body was warmed and loose, and her stretching was effortless.

One of the instructors wandered across to her. 'How's it going today?'

Vanessa straightened up and smiled. 'Great. I burned five hundred cals on the CV kit, I've just done fifty sit-ups without stopping, and my stretches are really good. I just seem so much more flexible—I must have really warmed my muscles.'

The instructor gave an answering smile. 'Sounds good— keep going! Unless you're pregnant, of course. If you are, we'll need to modify your programme over the coming months.'

Vanessa gave an astonished laugh. 'Pregnant? No, totally not.'

'OK,' the instructor returned easily, though he cast a quick professional glance at her midriff. 'I just mention it because you said you were feeling so flexible. Pregnancy softens your ligaments—preparing for birth and all that—so, although stretching gets easier, you have to be careful not to overdo it when you're pregnant.'

Vanessa gave another laugh and resumed her workout, not paying any more attention to the instructor's comment. She swept down from her waist, hands closing around her ankles, and started to pull her torso in towards her thighs. Yes, she mused, as she exerted increasing pressure on her calves to pull herself in more, she'd definitely gained a few pounds—she could feel a discernible bulge across her middle as she doubled over. Not much, but definitely more than there usually was.

Low-cal lunch today, my girl, she thought to herself. That bulge has got to go.

So, instead of going back up to the apartment after her workout, she went up to the health bar that accompanied the gym. Sipping sparkling water and eking out a small bowl of freshly prepared salad without dressing, she picked up one of the glossy magazines that were stashed on a rack, and started to flick through it.

Ten minutes later she was sitting stock still, salad unfinished, staring down at an article open in front of her. Her eyes were blank with shock.

It was one of those true-life articles, about a woman who had gone into labour in the middle of a department store not even knowing she was pregnant. One of those stories that always seemed so absurd—how could pregnancy be so unnoticeable?

Very easily, it seemed.

Vanessa stared again at the article, re-reading yet again the paragraph that had made the blood stop in her veins.

'I felt such a fool,' the woman was quoted as saying. 'I never knew antibiotics could mess up the Pill, and I assumed that because I went on having periods, even light ones, I obviously wasn't pregnant. I put my weight gain down to eating more, and when I threw up in the mornings I just thought I had a bug. I missed all the signs and I just couldn't believe it…'

Cold was snaking down Vanessa's back. No, this was some other woman entirely. A stranger. Nothing to do with her. Nothing.

I missed all the signs…

The words danced in front of her eyes. Imprinting themselves on her retina.

I just couldn't believe it…

And *I* don't believe it either, she thought urgently. I don't believe it because it isn't true. It's not true, and it can't be, and it isn't. I'm *not* pregnant, I don't feel pregnant, I don't look pregnant—

She shut her eyes. Fighting for sanity, for calm.

She would get a test, one of those kits from the chemist,

and that would set her mind at rest. No point getting into a tizz over an article about a complete stranger. A test would show her she was being idiotic. She would buy one that afternoon—no, straight away. To prove that of course, of *course,* she wasn't pregnant.

But what if you are?

The voice stabbed at her in her head. She crushed it instantly. She was not pregnant and that was all there was to it. She could not be pregnant. She just couldn't be.

It was impossible.

Replete, Markos ran his hand along the silken surface of Vanessa's bare thigh. He might be jet-lagged, he might be exhausted from a twenty-four-hour flight, landing him back in London at some ungodly hour of the morning, he might have a hectic schedule for the coming week and no chance of high-tailing it to the Caribbean for the next ten days at the earliest, but with Vanessa in his arms again he was not about to complain.

Christos, but she was good to come back to! Just knowing she was here, waiting for him, beautiful, sensual, adoring, had been compensation enough not just for the gruelling journey, but also for the excruciating evening he'd spent at his aunt's. She'd clearly been fully primed both by his father and Constantia Dimistris, and he'd had to use all his considerable finesse to parry the increasingly heavy-handed manipulation to get him to admit that, yes, he was prepared to succumb and take Apollonia Dimistris to wife.

'Oh, for heaven's sake, Markos, it will hardly be an ordeal!' his aunt had informed him exasperatedly. 'It's an excellent move. An alliance between Makarios and Dimistris wealth would be formidable. I wouldn't object to the girl for Leo, my own son, and if he won't snap her up then you certainly should! Whichever of you two marries her, her money will come into the Makarios family, and that's what counts.

'And if,' she'd challenged him, 'you and my son think that a wife would cramp your style when it comes to philandering—and heaven knows I can't decide which of you two is the worse!—then you can be sure it needn't. Your uncle took a new mistress a month after our honeymoon and I never objected. Why should I have? I'd become a Makarios, and providing my husband ensured I had a Makarios heir, that was all I required of him! Your own mother was a fool, kicking up such an unseemly fuss the way she did, and disgracing herself by flaunting her own lovers all over the place. Discretion, Markos, that is all that is required. Discretion. So...' Her eyes had rested on him knowingly. 'All you would need to do is either retire your current mistress and take a new one when Apollonia is decently pregnant, or, if you prefer, park your photogenic redhead—yes, I've seen those fashion shots!—in an apartment of her own until you can resume visiting her.'

Her expression had hardened suddenly.

'You're not thinking of *marrying* her, are you? Is *that* why you are being so stubborn about Apollonia Dimistris?'

Her voice had been sharp. His own had been even sharper.

'She's a mistress, that's all. And that is all, my dear aunt, that I require! *Not* a wife. Ever.' He'd thrown her a jaundiced look. 'With your marriage and my own parents' as examples, I think you can see why I feel that way.'

'Feelings?' His aunt had made a contemptuous noise in her throat. 'What on earth have feelings to do with it? We are talking about marriage, Markos, that is all. And it's time you saw sense about it!'

Now, safely back with Vanessa, he need not either see sense, as his father and his aunt defined it, or even waste his time thinking about something that was not going to happen.

His marriage.

To any woman.

Besides—his hand stroked softly, enticingly along Vanessa's silken flank—who needed marriage when there was such willing beauty to enjoy?

Slowly, savouringly, he caressed the soft swell of her abdomen. She was warm, and smooth, the contours of her body gently rounded. His hand travelled upwards, reaching the sweet swell of her breasts. He palmed them languorously. They felt full to his touch. Fuller than he remembered.

But all the more enticing for that.

Changing position, he shifted slightly and lowered his mouth. He heard her give a soft, helpless moan of pleasure. The sound, the sensual feel of her breasts beneath his grazing lips, aroused him more.

He felt his body respond, full and hard.

He moved over her.

Time to enjoy his homecoming.

'Close your eyes.'

Vanessa gazed up at Markos. Her body was still glowing from the bliss he had elicited from her.

'Go on, close them,' he repeated, brushing her mouth with his.

She let them close. Her heart-rate was still subsiding, her limbs still exhausted. She had given herself to him completely, absolutely, with an intensity that had blotted out everything else in existence. Everything else on her mind.

She felt his weight shift slightly, then a click, and then something cold was slithering over her skin. Her eyes flew open.

She gave a little cry.

'Oh Markos, they're *beautiful!*' she breathed, eyes wide.

'Opals from Australia. Each stone has a rainbow in its heart.' He draped the necklace around her throat. 'Exquisite,' he murmured. 'But never—' he dropped another soft, slow kiss on her mouth '—as exquisite as you.' He lifted his head to gaze into her dazed eyes. 'Every moment away from you was a torment,' he said softly.

Her face lit, glowing with happiness.

'Oh, Markos,' she breathed, 'do you mean it?'

He smiled down at her.

'Do you doubt it?' he asked, still in that caressing voice.

She shook her head, gazing up at him. 'No. Never. Oh, Markos!' She wrapped her arms around his back, holding him close to her.

They lay in each other's arms, wound about each other. A deep contentment filled him. Softly, he stroked her hair.

'Did you miss me?' he asked.

'Every minute!'

'Good.' He settled her more comfortably in the crook of his arm, feeling her head heavy on his chest. She fitted against him so well, he found himself thinking. Idly he splayed his hand over the sleek smoothness of her belly. Did she feel riper, rounder? He did not object. Skinny women did nothing for him, and Vanessa was definitely not skinny. Oh, no, she was all woman, all right …

And she was his—devotedly, absolutely.

The best mistress I've ever had.

Satisfaction eased through him again. The unpleasant scene with his aunt faded. It was so pointless, her and his father and Constantia Dimistris and the whole damn lot of them, scheming and plotting, going on and on at him—he was not going to marry and that was that. Nothing could get him to the altar.

He felt Vanessa shift her head very slightly on his chest.

'Markos?'

'Yes?' he murmured.

'Did—did *you* miss *me?*' There was the slightest hesitation in her voice as she asked the question.

He smiled, brushing her hair with his mouth.

'Didn't I just show you how much I missed you?'

She was silent a moment.

'Yes. But, I mean, was it...was it the sex you missed?'

He gave a low laugh. 'Well, I certainly didn't join the Mile High Club without you, I promise,' he answered lightly.

She was silent again.

'Markos?'

'Yes?' His encircling arm, cupping her shoulder, felt warm. Idly he twisted his fingers into her hair.

'What—what do you think is going to happen?'

He smiled. 'That's a pretty open-ended question. Care to narrow it down a bit? Are we talking about tomorrow's weather or the state of geopolitics?'

He could hear her swallow.

'I mean—about us.'

'Us?'

He felt her breath warm on his chest.

'Yes.'

'Well, like I said, as soon as I can get away we'll head for the Caribbean. Unless something comes up, of course,' he qualified. Business life could be unpredictable, and he didn't want to make promises he couldn't keep.

She was silent again. Then she spoke, in that same hesitant manner.

'I mean—in general—about us?'

The slightest prickle of irritation started up in him. He'd known women do this before—talking about 'us' in that way, making plans, forming expectations. False ones—they always were. He hoped to God that Vanessa weren't going to start on that. It was one of the things he appreciated most about her—that she simply went with the flow, the way he liked to do.

He gave an inward sigh. Maybe it was time to make that clear to her.

He shifted his weight, and her, so that she was tilted back to lie against the pillows. He lifted himself on to his elbow.

'Vanessa—what is this?'

She stared up at him. Something was flaring in her eyes, and he felt a momentary pang of guilt. She was so easy, never made demands, did everything he wanted and said, never made a fuss, never complained—went with the flow.

He could see her lips quiver.

His expression softened. Swiftly he lowered his mouth to kiss her briefly.

'Vanessa—we're having a great time. Don't let's get heavy about things, OK?'

She was staring up at him. Her eyes were huge. There was an expression in them he didn't like to see. It made him uncomfortable.

He firmed his lips, then spoke again.

'Vanessa, I appreciate having you around more than any other mistress I've ever had,' he told her. 'And I think I show my appreciation—don't I?' He lifted one of the opals set into the necklace looped around her neck.

Something shuttered in her eyes.

'You—you don't think I expect you to give me beautiful things, do you, Markos? Please don't think that. I couldn't bear it!'

'I like to give you beautiful things.'

'Yes, but you don't have to! Oh, Markos, you do believe that, don't you?'

There was such anxiety in her voice suddenly. He smiled. 'I told you—I like to give you things like this.'

'Yes, but—' She fell silent. She was gazing up at him, searching his face with troubled eyes. 'Markos…' Her voice was hesitant still. 'I…I'm not trying to be clingy, honestly. I know you'd hate that. It's just that…' Her voice trailed off.

Markos let go the necklace and took his hand away. He

didn't want this conversation. He seriously did not want it. But even more he did not want Vanessa returning to the subject another time. These things were best nipped in the bud. Another ripple of irritation went through him. A sense of ill-usage. Vanessa had seemed so different from the other women who'd tried this sort of thing on with him.

He didn't like to think she was the same as them. She'd been so different, all the time she'd been with him. Had someone been putting ideas in her head? His expression darkened momentarily.

Cosmo Dimistris. Was he responsible for this? Making her see that she could so easily pick herself another lover?

Even as the thought formed he felt a stab of rage go through him. *Thee mou,* no way was Vanessa going to pick herself another lover! She was *his*—and that was an end of it!

With instinctive possessiveness he lowered himself down off his elbow, sliding his arm around her again. That was better. Holding her felt good. He settled himself back comfortably against the pillows, positioning her against his shoulder, and felt his mood lift.

'Now you can cling all you like,' he said smilingly. He settled his free hand on her rounded stomach again, splaying out his fingers the way he liked to do. He felt her tense suddenly.

Was she worried about gaining weight? Worried he might not approve? He didn't want her thinking that.

'Don't panic,' he told her, amusement in his voice now. 'I like you soft and rounded—like a ripe peach.'

But his lightly spoken words did not seem to relax her. Maybe she was still upset from the exchange that had taken place? Well, there was nothing he could do about that. He lived his life on his own terms, nobody else's, and that was that.

And for the foreseeable future—for as far ahead as he was

prepared to look, and that wasn't far, because there was no reason to look further, he would live his life with Vanessa at his side. In his bed.

Maybe that was what was worrying her. Maybe she thought her shelf-life was up. Well, he could set her right on that, at any rate. He'd told her so before, that night she'd come up when he'd been speaking to the Duchesse—reassuring her that he still wanted her as his mistress. Clearly it was time to repeat the message.

He twisted his head slightly, so he could graze her brow with his mouth. It was a gesture of reassurance, possession. Then he spoke.

'Are you worried I'm getting bored with you? Is that it? If so, there's no need. I don't want you worrying, OK? I meant it when I said I missed you. I don't like it when I have to go away and, if you've noticed—' the slightest edge crept into his voice '—I tend not to do it unless it's unavoidable. Don't I take you with me everywhere?'

'Yes,' she answered in a low voice. 'You're very good to me, Markos. It's just that—'

'Yes?' The edge had sharpened an iota.

She must have registered it, because he saw that look fleet in her eyes again. But this time she did not relapse into silence. This time she spoke.

'Suppose something happens, Markos.'

His eyebrows rose.

'What sort of thing? Earth gets hit by an asteroid?'

She swallowed. 'No, I mean, like…something to us. Something that—that changes things.'

'Like you get tempted away to Mexico with another man on the strength of a dodgy promise of a cut-price emerald necklace?' he jibed gently, without rancour. He didn't like the way she'd got the conversation back to this subject.

But his attempt to steer her away from it failed.

He could feel her body tense in his arms. She wasn't looking at him, and he could see she'd shut her eyes.

'What sort of thing, Vanessa?' There was no humour in his voice, but no edge either. He kept it studiedly neutral. Sometimes that was the best way to flush out what someone was trying to say.

Or conceal.

Suddenly, with the kind of certainty that came to him when he was in a business negotiation and he knew that his opponent was making a feint of some kind, Markos knew that Vanessa was about to get evasive.

Well, he wasn't having that. She was the one who'd turned the conversation heavy. Now she could follow it through.

'What sort of thing?' he repeated, keeping the same neutral tone in his voice.

He felt her swallow again.

'Nothing,' she said. 'Honestly—nothing.'

Why did women do that? thought Markos, suppressing the irritation that had sliced through him again at her response. Why did they start to say something, then say 'nothing' in that tone?

'Vanessa?' He wanted this sorted—now. He really wasn't in the mood for it—it wasn't the kind of conversation he'd ever been in the mood for—and coming right now, when his body and mind were replete and relaxed, when he'd just spent days travelling to the other side of the world and back again, and getting hassled by his aunt while he was there, it was definitely not what he wanted.

But it had to be done. It wasn't a topic he wanted to come up a second time.

'You can't just say "nothing" like that, and then go silent on me.'

He could feel the tension stiffen her body, but he hardened his heart. This had to be sorted, or it would just louse things

up further down the line, and that was the last thing he wanted.
Life with Vanessa was too good for him to want it to do that.

'So? What sort of thing?' he prompted.

There was a long—overlong—pause. Then, finally, she
answered him.

She'd opened her eyes, and was looking straight at him,
tension and apprehension in their amber depths.

'Supposing I got pregnant,' she said.

CHAPTER SEVEN

FOR A LONG moment, there was complete silence. Then, very, very carefully, Markos spoke.

'*Are* you pregnant?'

The neutrality in his voice was absolute.

But it cost him every ounce of effort. His mind had slammed shut. Totally shut. It was essential.

He heard her take a breath.

Was it him, or did the breath seem to take for ever?

Then—'No,' she answered.

He felt relief sheet out, like a flash flame through his consciousness.

'But...' She was speaking again. 'But if I were, what... what would...what...?'

'But you're not.' His voice was flat. Inside, he was nailing something down, very hard, very instant. 'So idle speculation of this kind is pointless. Especially since you are not going to get pregnant—are you, Vanessa?'

He looked straight at her, into those wide, expressionless eyes.

Too expressionless?

He felt that thing he'd nailed down so fast, so hard, strain against him, but he ignored it. Instead, he directed every ounce of his mental focus on to what he said next.

'If you're concerned about your current method of contraception it can be changed. Go to the doctor this afternoon and sort something else.' He made a heroic effort to inject a lighter note into this conversation from hell. 'I'll even put up with condoms if it makes you happy. Now, isn't that a sacrifice?' He forced a smile to his lips.

But she didn't smile back. Her eyes were still staring at him, still quite expressionless.

A shaft of annoyance speared through him.

Though he didn't want to, he knew it was time to get tough. And that annoyed him even more. Never in all the time Vanessa had been with him had he thought he was going to have to have one of these damn conversations with her. He'd thought she knew better.

Evidently not.

Maybe all women were the same, after all, whatever the appearances to the contrary.

He sat up, reaching for the bathrobe he'd abandoned after showering when he'd got back from the airport. Standing up, he shrugged it on, and belted the tie.

Then he stood, looking down at her, so he could get the message across. He didn't want to do it, but it had to be done. God, who knew better than him that it had to be done?

He took a sharp intake of breath and began.

'Vanessa, I've told you this before—you're the best mistress I've ever had, and I appreciate you considerably. *But—*' His eyes bored down into hers, nailing home the message. 'This is a very big but, and you have to take it on board—I am *not* going to marry you. Under any circumstances. So, please, do not try and bargain with a child's life in order to achieve that end. Because if I have the slightest suspicion that you are trying to play that game then you are out. OK? Totally out. No hesitation, no second chances. Nothing. *Out.*'

For one long, level moment he stood, looking down at her where she lay in his bed, ripe from his lovemaking.

Her face was expressionless.

So was his.

'Out,' he repeated, the warning sounding like a hammer blow.

Then, turning on his heel, he stalked into the *en suite* bathroom.

There was an old black and white movie playing on the huge plasma screen TV in the lounge, but Vanessa wasn't watching it. She was staring at the flickering images, but she wasn't seeing them.

She wasn't doing anything, except sitting, curled up on the sofa, while the rain beat on the closed terrace windows, the wind buffeted the high penthouse apartment.

Markos was gone. Gone to his offices in the City, whisked away in his chauffeured car, the faithful Taki and Stelios in attendance as usual. A rich man, with a rich man's things to do.

She stared ahead of her.

And what am I? she thought. The answer tolled in her brain like a funeral bell.

A rich man's mistress.

One of the many luxuries a rich man acquired to make his life pleasant and enjoyable.

That's all I am to him. I'll never, never be anything else...

His mistress.

Her eyes stared unseeingly ahead.

Didn't he tell me? Didn't he say it often enough—that horrible afternoon with the emeralds from that disgusting Cosmo Dimistris? Mistress, mistress, mistress.

The word tolled through her, would not be silenced.

I tried to pretend it didn't matter, that it was only a word, that it was how he treated me that was more important. But

all along it was just as a mistress that he was treating me—
someone for his bed, to pamper and indulge and amuse
himself with.

Nothing more than that.

Nothing more than a mistress.

Her body was immobile, curled up on the huge sofa, and she'd been sitting there for ever, it seemed, while her brain went round and round.

He thinks I want to get him to marry me. That I'm trying to trap him into marriage with pregnancy.

She felt her stomach hollow out, the breath solidifying in her lungs.

Her whole body felt as if it was slowly freezing.

The low buzz of the doorbell did not register at first. But when it was repeated it managed to penetrate her numbed senses.

Slowly, very slowly, she got to her feet. She'd been immobile for so long that the blood was not flowing properly to her feet, and it took her a moment to make herself walk jerkily towards the door. Whatever it was, whatever was being delivered, she did not want it.

But the bell buzzed again, insistently, and with numbed, stumbling legs she went to answer it.

It wasn't a delivery.

It was a middle-aged woman she'd never seen in her life.

Vanessa opened her mouth to say, 'May I help you?' gathering her stricken thoughts to try and be civil, but the woman simply walked inside, her bulk carrying her forwards. Vanessa, utterly taken aback, could only blink.

Gaining the entrance hall, the woman turned.

'I wish to speak to you.'

Vanessa's brain was like porridge. All she registered was that the woman was expensively dressed, had Mediterranean colouring, and spoke English with an accent—and in the kind of tones that, Vanessa knew from her time with Markos, rich people reserved for those who were not rich.

The woman's eyes flickered over her. They were dark, and not friendly.

Hostile.

Vanessa swallowed. Who was this woman? And why had she just barged in here? And why had the concierge not phoned to first to ask if she could come up?

The woman's eyes flicked over her in that same hostile manner. Then, again without waiting for an invitation, she walked through into the lounge.

'Turn that off,' she instructed, gesturing at the TV.

Silently, Vanessa crossed to the coffee table and clicked the remote. The room fell silent. She turned. This woman might be rude, but she would not be.

'I'm sorry,' she began, 'but I don't know—'

'I am Constantia Dimistris,' the woman announced, in accented, haughty tones.

'Dimistris?' Vanessa echoed the name. Then, with a shock, she realised that she did, after all, recognise the woman. It had been a fleeting moment, but she was the older of the two women who had walked out of the lift at the hotel where that party had been held. The party where the odious Cosmos Dimistris had accosted her.

Dimistris? Was she something to do with that creep? Was this woman his wife? No, not his wife—she was a generation older—fifty rather than thirty. So—who?

'I will not mince my words—I see no point in doing so.'

The woman was speaking in a tone that indicated that Vanessa was one of the unwashed masses. She had opened a red lacquer designer handbag and was taking out a piece of paper which she dropped on the coffee table.

'It is post-dated,' the woman informed her. 'I am not un-reasonable. I give you two weeks. That should be ample time.'

Vanessa swallowed again. What on earth was going on? Why was this middle-aged woman who might—or might not—be Cosmo Dimistris's mother here? She picked up the piece of paper.

It was a cheque, made out for twenty-five thousand pounds, the payee name left blank.

'I don't understand,' Vanessa said faintly.

The woman made an irritated noise in her throat.

'Do not be obtuse. I do not wish to be here any longer than is necessary. You can see quite clearly what the amount on the cheque is, and the date. You will get not a penny more, I assure you, if that is what you are thinking of! That is simple enough to understand, no?'

Vanessa could only stare. This was quite mad. Was it something to do with Cosmo Dimistris's horrible attentions to her?

'Mrs Dimistris,' she began, 'if this is something to do with…with, um, Cosmo Dimistris—'

The woman's eyes flashed in outrage.

'*What?* Why do you mention my son?' she demanded. 'What have you been up to? Importuning him?'

She sounded so indignant that for a moment Vanessa wanted to slap her. So Cosmo *was* her son—and she had the nerve to think he had been the innocent party!

'On the contrary,' she said coldly. 'Your son—as I take it he is—behaved in a manner that any woman would find despicable. I am sorry to say that, but it is true.'

The woman bridled. 'How dare someone like *you* make such an accusation?'

Vanessa's lips pressed together.

'Because it was *I* who was on the receiving end! If you imagine it is pleasant to be invited to become a man's mistress, to be sent an emerald bracelet as persuasion, then I assure you that you are mistaken!'

The woman's bosom heaved and her eyes flashed.

'You refused him?' she demanded.

'Of course I did!' Vanessa retorted. She wanted the woman to go—and go now.

But Constantia Dimistris's eyes only narrowed speculatively.

'So you were already holding out for more. I should have known. Well!' Her head reared up. 'That cheque is the only money on the table—it will not be increased, whatever your wiles. And do not think that my son will repeat his offer. I happen to know that he has taken a very beautiful model to Mexico only last week!' She announced this as if it were some kind of triumphant put-down for Vanessa.

A hysterical desire to laugh almost overcame Vanessa. It was like being in the middle of some bizarre farce.

But it was one entirely without humour. Whoever this woman was, whatever the reason she had barged in here, her words, attitude and behaviour were insupportable.

Vanessa held out the cheque.

'Please take this back. I have no idea why you are trying to give it to me, and I must ask that you leave.'

She spoke in a quiet, dignified fashion. She would not reduce herself to the other woman's level.

But she might as well have been speaking to herself. Constantia Dimistris's face hardened, and she made no attempt either to take the cheque or to move.

'You are insolent! But I did not come here to bandy words. I came here—which I need not have done, be assured!— simply to make your departure easier. To spare you—' her expression did not match her words '—from the necessity of being given your marching orders by Markos Makarios.'

Vanessa's face bleached.

'What on earth are you talking about?'

A look of cold pleasure showed in the woman's eyes.

'So you did not know? He has kept you in complete ignorance.' The malice in her voice was quite open.

'About?' said Vanessa. Her arm, holding out the cheque, dropped to her side.

Constantia Dimistris lifted her chin and looked at her disdainfully, with mock pity in her eyes.

'Your time is up. Very shortly you will need to seek a new protector. Hence my offer to expedite your departure.' She nodded at the cheque hanging limply from Vanessa's nerveless fingers.

Vanessa forced herself to speak. 'I really have absolutely no idea what you are talking about.'

Malice—and satisfaction—mingled in the woman's voice and eyes.

'Allow me to enlighten you, in that case. In a very short space of time Markos Makarios will have no need of a mistress and will dispose of you. You see...' there was a note of absolute satisfaction and triumph in her voice '...he will shortly be marrying my daughter.'

Pain. Grief. Despair. Laced together, like stitches running through a gaping wound in her flesh, with disbelief.

It couldn't be true. What that horrible, horrible woman had thrown at her—it couldn't be.

Markos, getting married. To a Greek girl, the daughter of that woman. The last ugly remnants of her visit rang in Vanessa's ears. She had taken such malicious delight in telling Vanessa, and discovering her ignorance had seemed to elicit a particular relish. She had departed on an openly triumphant note.

'You can ply your trade elsewhere from now on. The power of a mistress is nothing, *nothing* compared with the power of a wife! I know your sort.' Her lip had curled sneeringly. 'Opening your legs to every man and—'

'Please leave.' Vanessa's voice had been level, but inside she'd been falling. Falling from the greatest height.

She had crossed to the front door and opened it, standing

by it pointedly. For a moment the woman had simply stood, eyes flashing with malice and hostility, then she had swept forward, and out into the corridor beyond.

Vanessa had closed the door behind her, her whole body trembling. How she'd made it back to the sofa she did not know.

And all she'd been able to do was collapse on it and sit there, as she was torn apart.

Outside, the rain lashed down with pitiless ferocity.

After a long, long while, as the overcast daylight began to fail, she got slowly, very slowly, to her feet. She made her way into one of the spare bedrooms and opened the closet. Her suitcases were inside.

Lifting them as if they were dead weights, even though they were empty, she made her way to the master bedroom.

It took her a long time to pack.

Markos's mobile rang. He answered it immediately.

'Well?' His voice barked harshly.

'It wasn't her, sir.'

'You're sure?'

Taki's voice came over the ether, sounding studiedly neutral.

'Kyrios Dimistris's companion is a model by the name of Sylva Ramboulli.' He paused for a fraction. 'The agent there took photos of them together, if you wish to see them.'

'No, damn you! But if she's not with—'

His voice broke off, then resumed.

'Keep looking,' he said tersely. He didn't wait for an answer, just cut the connection.

He sat at his desk, staring out across his vast office. Every muscle in his body was motionless, tense.

Three days. Three days since he'd come back that evening to an apartment that had been strangely, eerily silent. Different.

He'd come back before when Vanessa hadn't yet been back from whatever she did in the daytime. But it had not been the same. Something had been different the moment he'd walked in. He had felt it.

He'd gone into his bedroom to change out of his suit, and then taken a shower. It had been in the *en suite* bathroom as he was drying himself, that he'd noticed. It had looked—different. He'd gone back out into the bedroom. That had looked different too. For a moment he hadn't been able to work out what it was, then it had registered. There was nothing on the bedside table on Vanessa's side of the bed. Usually there was a book, or a tube of handcream. Maybe she'd had a tidying blitz.

He'd gone into the closet to select some clothes to relax in for the evening. He'd wanted a quiet evening in—the jet lag had been catching up with him, and he'd wanted nothing more than to relax and chill out.

Make his peace with Vanessa.

He shouldn't have spoken to her like that, he knew it. Oh, not the message—the message had had to be got across—but he could have put it more gently. But her challenge to him had come out of the blue, he'd been totally unprepared for it. Hell, it was one he'd never expected Vanessa, of all women, to make! He'd thought he was safe with her—that she was different.

Well, she *was* different—six months of her had confirmed it. No other woman had ever been as devoted, as adoring as Vanessa. But it was exactly that devotion that had made him think that she would never try anything on with him.

Words had played in his memory. Leo at his *schloss,* putting his arm around his shoulder one morning, just before they set out on the day's skiing trip. Speaking to him in a warning tone.

'You've got a mistress in a million, but never forget, little cousin, that naivety can be as dangerous as cunning. Watch yourself with her.'

He'd only laughed. 'How was your sable beauty last night? As good as she looks?'

Leo had dropped his arm immediately. His expression had been grim and his voice even harsher as he'd said, 'Leave it.'

Markos had thrown up a hand. 'OK, OK. You sort your own problems out.'

Leo's eyes had flashed. 'You may have some of your own,' he'd thrown at him, and stalked off, bad mood clearly visible.

Markos had looked after him pityingly. He didn't have problems, not with Vanessa. That was why he'd kept her so long. Because she never gave him any grief.

As the conversation had replayed itself in his memory, Markos had felt his expression harden. His cousin had been right. Vanessa's naivety had proved a problem after all.

Because naivety, Markos knew, was what it was. What she'd thrown at him that morning after his return from Australia had not been an attempt at manipulation, an exercise in female cunning. He accepted that now. He hadn't at the time. He'd gone into knee-jerk reaction, his brain out of kilter from jet lag, and laid into her. But even before he'd reached the office he'd begun regretting his reaction. He should have been easier on her. Spelt it out, yes. But not so brutally.

She was naïve, that was all. He'd hurt her. He'd seen it in her face.

It hadn't made him feel good.

And he didn't like not feeling good.

He'd decided he would get his PA to deliver flowers—a lot of flowers—and take that hurt look out of her face.

But he'd never got around to giving the instruction. The moment he'd walked into his office he'd been bombarded with a dozen more urgent things to attend to, and somewhere along the rest of the day he'd forgotten all about it. Instead, as Taki had driven him back to the apartment early that evening, he'd intended to take the hurt look out of her face in person. He'd sit her down, take her hand, and explain—kindly, gently, but firmly—why she must understand that he liked his life just the way it was. That she was the best mistress he'd ever had, that he really appreciated her, and that they would make it to the Caribbean the very first moment he could get away.

But to do all that she'd have had to be there. And she hadn't. As he'd walked through into his closet to change into casual clothes he'd been on the edge of feeling a flicker of irritation at her. OK, so maybe she was just out buying a new dress, or getting her hair done or whatever—maybe she'd thought that wowing him that night would be the best way to get past the episode that morning—but her timing was bad. Here he was, all prepared to kiss and make up, and she wasn't around.

He had walked into the closet—and stopped dead.

Definitely different. His eyes had raced round. There had still been a rackful of her clothes hanging on her side but it had looked thinner somehow. His eyes had gone to her vanity unit. It had been cleared of all her stuff. He didn't know what the stuff was exactly, but it took up a lot of space: bottles and pots and tubes and God knew what. They hadn't been there. Without realising what he was doing he had pulled open one of her drawers at random.

It had been empty.

He'd opened another one. That had had some designer lingerie in it, the next was empty again. He'd opened her shoe cupboard—again, there had been shoes there, but fewer of them. He'd stared a moment, then something else had registered. The pair of worn house-sandals she loved to wear—and that he always wanted her to throw away because they were so worn out—had gone.

Realisation had dawned through him—and relief. She'd had a clear-out. That was what she'd done. The typical reaction of a woman under stress—defragging her wardrobe so she could restock it.

The tension had ebbed from him, and as it had, he'd realised just how tense he'd been.

Light-hearted again, now that he'd figured what she'd done—of course she was still shopping to replace what she'd chucked out—he had changed into casual clothes and headed out to the lounge to help himself to a beer. He'd felt he needed one.

But by nine that evening he had realised he needed more than beer. He needed Vanessa—and she hadn't come back yet. Relief had turned to irritation long ago, but now irritation was turning to concern.

By midnight concern had become a deep, gut-wrenching fear.

His entire personal security staff had been on the case by then, checking police and hospitals and taxi firms. The concierge who had summoned a taxi for her mid-afternoon had been grilled repeatedly, but had been able to give no more information. Nor had the taxi driver who'd been traced. He'd dropped Vanessa off in Oxford Street and that was that.

She'd been carrying a suitcase, but that hadn't bothered Markos. It would simply have contained the clothes she was getting rid of. He already knew that she never threw stuff away—if he told her he'd gone off an outfit, she gave it to a charity shop.

By noon the next day however Markos had known, with a dull, bleak fury that the suitcase had not contained old clothes for charity shops.

Vanessa had run out on him.

When the realisation had finally dawned on him, when no other explanation was possible, despite his best effort to come up with one, his fury had been absolute. What the *hell* did she think she was playing at? Six months with him and she walked out without a word? *Christos,* he deserved better than that! OK, so he'd been a bit hard on her that last morning—but what the hell reason was that for flouncing out in a huff, for God's sake? It was out of all proportion to react that badly!

Unless she'd needed an excuse to leave….

The thought had come like a cold knife-blade in his guts.

Cosmo Dimistris and his offer to take her over and fly her out to Mexico.

No! Every atom in his body had rejected the idea. This was Vanessa, not some ambitious, gold-digging chancer who traded protectors at the drop of her knickers! Nor was she an experienced sophisticate who selected men according to their bank balance and social circle. This was Vanessa. *His* Vanessa.

Who'd just walked out on him.

The knife had twisted savagely.

Grimly, he'd ordered Taki to follow through on Cosmo Dimistris. If she *had* gone off to him, he'd… He didn't know what he'd do, but it would be savage. As savage as the feelings stabbing through him.

But it wasn't her with Cosmo in Mexico. The relief he felt as he disconnected was brief. Where the hell was she?

And why the hell had she gone?

His security team had turned up nothing. Nothing at all. He'd cursed them for incompetents, then accepted that they had nothing, after all, to go on. Her last sighting had been in Oxford Street, late afternoon, the day he'd arrived back from Australia.

Since then Vanessa had disappeared off the face of the earth.

Markos had ordered his team to leave no stone unturned, but when he'd been asked for mundane details, like her home address, place of birth, date of birth, he'd realised, with a strange, chill feeling, that he hadn't the faintest idea. In the early days, in Paris, Vanessa had talked of her background and family circumstances, but she hadn't, to his best recollection, mentioned the town she'd grown up in, or given her address. His security team had had to start from scratch with her name, tracing it through electoral rolls and registers of births. They'd found an address for her, all right, but it was no longer valid. It hadn't been since before Christmas. The house had been sold early in December, and though the new owners had given him the name of the conveyancing solicitors, the latter had no address for the seller other than that of the house itself and, ironically, the address of his own Chelsea apartment. Enquiries of neighbours and all other possible avenues had given no information as to where Vanessa might now be.

No one knew.

Least of all him.

He went on staring out over his office.

Keep looking, he'd told Taki. But was there any point? Vanessa had gone because she'd wanted to go, that was all.

She'd had no good reason, but she'd gone all the same.

Gone.

The word went through Markos's brain again.

Gone.

It was a very final word.

The sound of his mobile ringing jarred him, and he seized it from where he'd dropped it on the mahogany surface of his desk.

'Yes?' His voice was a bark.

An amused laugh was his answer. 'You sound stressed, little cousin.'

'Leo?'

'Who else? Tell me, can you make lunch?'

'Today?'

'Yes.'

'I didn't know you were in London. Listen, this is not a good time right now.' He hung up unceremoniously.

He didn't want Leo around. He didn't want lunch. He wanted Vanessa, and she'd walked out on him.

He went back to staring out across his office.

Half an hour later the door to his PA's office opened and Leo strolled in. There was a tall, dark-haired, stunning woman with him whom Markos half recognised.

He got to his feet, exasperation in his face. 'Leo, I said this wasn't a good time—'

His cousin ignored him.

'We're flying to Athens this afternoon, so this is my only opportunity.' He paused, drawing the woman forward. Markos's eyes flickered over her, then back to Leo. His expression was still not welcoming.

His cousin was ignoring his lack of warmth.

'I stopped by deliberately. I wanted you to be the first of the family to congratulate me. Probably the only one.'

Markos looked at him blankly. 'Congratulate you?'

Leo grinned, throwing a glance at the woman beside him, who returned it with a smile. For a second something went through Markos that made him feel hollow. Leo's good humour was like sandpaper on his skin.

His cousin's next words were a bolt from the blue.

'I'm married,' said Leo, and grinned.

Markos just stared, disbelievingly.

'You're *what?*'

His cousin's grin widened.

'You heard me, little cousin. This is Anna—remember Anna? Gave me a hard time in Austria? Well—she finally saw sense and fell for me. Couldn't resist me!'

'More fool me!' the woman at his side retorted.

Leo dropped a kiss on her forehead. 'She adores me,' he said confidingly to his cousin.

Anna rolled her eyes. 'Definitely more fool me.' But the smile was still on her face as she said it.

Markos could say nothing, only stare.

Leo nodded at his new wife.

'Takes a lot to silence my little cousin, but looks like I've succeeded.' He turned his attention back to Markos. 'You can come and kiss the bride—but only on the cheek. I get the rest of her! She's too fantastic to waste on anyone but me.'

Anna raised her brows mock-wearily. 'He can't help himself,' she explained to Markos.

'You're married,' Markos said again, as if he needed to repeat it to believe it.

Leo strolled over to the drinks cabinet in the office, pulled it open as if it belonged to him, and extracted a bottle of champagne from the fridge.

'Signed, sealed and delivered,' he agreed, deftly opening the bottle. He poured out three foaming glassfuls and handed them around. Markos took his numbly. His cousin settled himself down in one of the pair of large wing chairs and pulled his wife down on his knee. She draped an arm around his neck and started to sip her champagne.

Leo lifted his glass.

'To marriage,' he said, and drank. 'Don't stand there looking like you're chewing a lemon—drink up!' He took another mouthful and cast a benevolent eye on Markos.

'I've come with a message, little cousin. Remember at the Levantsky launch? Me warning you about Vanessa adoring you? Well, I've wised up. An adoring woman is the best thing a man can have. I should know—I've got one of my own, and she thinks the sun shines out of my—ouch!' He winced exaggeratedly as Anna punched his shoulder warningly.

Markos watched the byplay expressionlessly. He felt as if a train were running over him.

'Vanessa's left me.'

The words were out before he could stop them.

It was like a freeze frame. Leo's champagne flute stalled in mid-lift. Anna stilled on his knee, her hand still playfully fisted.

'She's left you?' It was Leo's turn to echo his cousin dumbly.

Anna got to her feet.

'*Vanessa* left *you?*' she said. 'But she was completely nuts on you.'

'She walked out three days ago.'

Leo's face was sober. 'What happened? Why did she go?'

Markos looked away. 'I have no idea.' He drew in a sharp breath and deposited his unwanted champagne glass on his desk with a click. 'She had no reason to,' he went on. His voice sounded strange in his own ears, harsh, but very remote. 'She had everything she wanted with me. Everything. She was the best mistress I ever had—'

There was another sharp inhalation of breath. But not from him.

'*Mistress?*' Anna's voice cut like a knife.

'Uh-oh,' said Leo.

Markos stiffened at the open aggression in Anna's voice. He glanced coolly at her. Anna's face was darkening.

'You regarded Vanessa as your *mistress?*' she demanded.

Leo began to say, 'I should explain—' in Greek. His wife twisted her head.

'Don't let him off the hook! God, *he's* the one with the English mother! He's got *no* excuse for talking like that!' She turned her wrath back on Markos, her eyes snapping with anger.

'You know, I always thought Vanessa was a fool to be so besotted with you—because obviously you weren't about to make all her dreams come true, were you? I always knew it was going to be tears before bedtime for her. But I didn't realise what a total louse you were! You actually have the gall to stand there and insult her like this—calling her your *mistress!*'

'Anna—' Leo's voice was temporising.

She turned on him, snapping, 'Don't you *dare* take his side!' then whipped back to Markos. 'If Vanessa's finally seen sense and walked out on you then I say thank God for

that. She can do a whole lot better than a jerk like you! Leo.'
She glared at him. 'I want to go. Now.'

She stormed out, not waiting to see if Leo was following.

'What the hell—?' said Markos slowly.

His cousin shrugged heavily and reverted to Greek.

'Bad word to use—mistress. Doesn't go down well.'

'Why the hell not? What's their problem?'

Leo just looked at him.

'Maybe, little cousin, one day you'll wise up and find out.'
His voice was dry and sombre, but it held a note of something
in it that Markos had never heard before from Leo.

Pity.

Markos stiffened. He didn't need pity. And certainly not
from his cousin. A cousin who'd quite clearly lost his marbles.

'Why on earth have you gone and got married?' he
demanded.

For a moment Leo's eyes narrowed belligerently. Then, deliberately, he calmed.

'Marriage can work, Markos. There *are* good marriages in
this world. I'm proof of that.'

Markos threw him a jaundiced look. 'Honeymoons are the
easy bit,' he said. 'It's what comes after that screws it up. And
screws up anyone who gets trapped in the middle.'

The look of pity came again in Leo's eyes.

'You got a raw deal, I know,' he said quietly. 'But you don't
have to damn the whole game just because of it—'

'It's best to just stay clear of it, that's all,' finished Markos.
'Which I have every intention of doing.' He straightened his
shoulders. 'Look, I'm not in the mood right now for any of
this. If you've gone and got yourself married, I'm staying out
of it—just let me know when you need a good divorce lawyer,
and I'll find you the best.'

Leo shook his head and gave a resigned laugh.

'I won't need one. Listen, little cousin.' His voice changed.

'I'm sorry about Vanessa. More than I can say. If ever a woman thought the sun shone out of you, she did. Whatever went wrong, I hope you can fix it.'

For a moment Markos's eyes were bleak. Then his mouth tightened.

'Maybe it's just not worth fixing,' he said. 'Maybe I should just damn her to hell and be done with it. I'll get along just fine without her.'

Leo looked at him. Looked at the tension webbing his eyes, the tic high in his cheekbone, the haggard look around his mouth.

'Yeah—right,' he said.

CHAPTER EIGHT

'IT'S MRS DIMISTRIS again, Mr Makarios,' Markos's PA said apologetically down the line to him as he picked up the phone in his office.

An expletive was instantly suppressed.

'Put her through,' said Markos grimly. This was not the first time Constantia Dimistris had phoned, but it was the first time he'd spoken to her. Time to get rid of her permanently.

'Constantia,' he said levelly, as he was put through.

The conversation that followed was neither brief nor pleasant. But it was at least, Markos hoped, effective. In the end he was reduced to bluntness.

'Apollonia is a lovely girl, but further acquaintance would be pointless. Whatever my father may have led you to believe—and please accept my profound regrets if that is indeed the case—I am not considering marriage. Please, therefore, stop considering me as a prospective son-in-law. Apollonia deserves a man who can give her the devotion that any wife should have.'

Even as he said the courteous words he knew they were, however unintentionally, tactless. It was well known that Constantia Dimistris's late husband had been notoriously *un*-devoted to his wife, mounting a stable of mistresses and taking them everywhere with him. She was as bitter about her own marriage as she was ambitious for her daughter's. As for poor Apollonia—well, maybe she would do better with her mother's next target.

Memory stabbed at him as he hung up. The night that Cosmo Dimistris had so signally failed to warn him that his mother and sister were staying at the same hotel. Apollonia had gazed with open fascination at Vanessa. With her sheltered upbringing she would never have seen a man's mistress before.

Markos's eyes hardened.

What the hell was wrong with calling Vanessa his mistress? It was what she had been. There was no shame in it. She had lived with him, *ergo* she had been his mistress.

No—he didn't want to think about Vanessa. Didn't want to remember her. She was gone. She'd made her choice, and that choice had been to walk out on him. In the many long weeks since she'd left, he'd come to terms with that. He'd had no choice.

She didn't want him any more. End of story. He wasn't going to chase after a woman who didn't want him.

If ever a woman thought the sun shone out of you, she did...

Leo's words echoed in his head. He thrust them out. He'd thought Vanessa devoted—well, now he knew better.

He sat back in his chair and flicked open the leather folder on his desk. It was an acquisitions proposal, and it looked highly profitable. He looked down at the figures, narrowing his focus.

They blurred in front of his eyes.

Mouth tightening, he forced himself to concentrate. He was flying to Geneva that evening, and he had no time to waste. Two days in Geneva, and then it was Boston. Then Jo'burg. Then Sydney, and back to Frankfurt. Then Paris. Then New York.

These days he liked to keep busy.

* * *

Markos pushed back against the leather seat in the first-class cabin, flexing his shoulders restlessly. Tiredness seeped through him—he had been on the go for ever, it seemed, and he'd crossed so many time-zones his body-clock was totally haywire—yet he could not sleep. Outside through the porthole the dark, moonless night, high above the cloud base, reached into infinity. Around him, the low vibration of powerful jet engines hummed. The cabin lights were low, interspersed here and there with the pools of reading lights.

He was in no mood to read. No mood to work at his laptop. No mood to watch the in-flight entertainment on the screen in front of him.

No mood to do anything except look out over the formless night, his face shuttered, inexpressive.

Damn her.

Damn her to hell and back.

He'd been going to put her behind him. Forget all about her. Move on. There were women galore in the world he inhabited— beautiful, eager, exquisite. A host of them to choose from.

The moment he'd showed up at his first social affair without Vanessa—not that he'd wanted to go, but it had been predominantly a business occasion and he'd had no choice— they'd made a beeline for him. Beautiful, sophisticated, sexy—all eager to catch his interest, his attention.

He hadn't wanted any of them. Not one.

It wasn't just that same sense of *ennui* that had assailed him in Paris last year. That sense of searching for novelty that was increasingly hard to find as the years went by.

Ennui was nothing compared to what he was going through now.

This mix of emotions was poisonous. Anger, a bitter sense of ill-usage, sheer incomprehension as to why she had walked out on him without a word—and lacing all through it something that was much worse. Something he didn't, wouldn't, give a name to, but which ate at him like a cancer.

With a rough gesture he picked up the copy of the *Wall Street Journal* that had been handed out by the flight attendant. He looked at it cursorily. He was in no mood for reading about the global economic situation, the complex manoeuvrings of companies and governments and central banks. He tossed the paper aside. Surely to God something could distract him?

Moodily he reached for the glass of whisky that was on the table at his side, and took a mouthful of the burning liquid. Then he put that aside too. Getting drunk was no answer. He'd done that several times in these last bitter few months, and had regretted it every time. The oblivion was only temporary, and the emotions that the lowering of his defences allowed to rip through him were devastating.

His mouth tightened. The woman who'd walked out on him without a word, a reason, wasn't worth a single hangover.

He shifted again restlessly.

He wanted her.

Vanessa. He wanted her here, at his side. He wanted to be able to glance at her, let his eyes rest on her extraordinary beauty, let his gaze wander over her, take in the line of her profile, the glory of her hair, the soft, sweet curves of her body. Knowing that when they had reached their destination, wherever in the world it was, he would take her straight to bed....

No! Don't think about that! Don't think about having Vanessa in his arms, his bed, how her ardour had inflamed him, how his passion for her had consumed him...

We were so good together—what the hell did she have to walk out on me for? Why did she do it?

He stared blindly in front of him.

There was no answer. None. She had gone, and that was that.

And he simply didn't know why.

With a sharp inward sigh, of anger and bleakness, he yanked the in-flight magazine from its pocket. He started to flick through it, not caring what was in it, totally uninterested, just wanting anything to distract him.

And then, abruptly, he stopped flicking and just stared.

It was Vanessa.

Her photograph, looking out of the page at him, her beauty so incandescent that he felt scorched by it.

Utterly still, he gazed at the page, taking in every detail of her face in the image. He felt his insides clench, and the cancer clawed at him with its savage, merciless pincers.

What the hell is she doing in a magazine?

He forced his eyes away from her face, flicking rapidly over the page. It was an advert for some designer he'd never heard of.

What is she doing in an advert?

He forced his brain to work.

She must have taken a job as a model. Something must have come up after that publicity shoot she'd done for Leo's launch of the Levantsky jewels.

Was that why she'd left? She'd been offered a contract and snapped it up—dumping him in the process?

The anger stabbed through him again. Why would she have left him just because she'd been offered a modelling contract? *Christos,* he wouldn't have objected! She had been perfectly welcome to do whatever amused her during the daytime—he wouldn't have said no. OK, he wouldn't have wanted her travelling abroad without him, but apart from that she would have been welcome to start a modelling career if that was what she was keen on. All she'd have had to do was ask him—he'd have gladly said yes.

A surge of bitter ill-usage bit through him. No, she'd had to go and make some kind of dramatic exit, disappear into the night, walk out on him without a word.

Damn her to hell for it!

His eyes went back to the image on the page, taunting him with her beauty—her utterly unobtainable beauty.

And finally something registered, slowly, like a wave welling from far, far away. The words of the script accompanying the photo blurred and swirled and then cleared.

And left him rigid with shock.

Vanessa set down her brush in the paint tray and surveyed her handiwork so far. A faint smile lit her face. She was glad she was capable of it—smiles were as rare as hens' teeth these days.

But the primrose yellow walls looked bright and cheerful in the afternoon light, even though the room on this side of the house lost the sunlight after lunchtime. She stood for a moment, admiring the transformation of the hitherto dark walls, absently rubbing the small of her back. She knew she'd been somewhat ambitious in attempting to paint walls at this stage, but she also knew it was a case of now or never. With the walls done she could get the new carpet delivered, as well as move the new furniture in. Fortunately, the rest of the house was in good decorative order, and she had been able to move in the moment the sale had gone through.

House-hunting, the buying process, and moving and settling in had all kept her busy over the past weeks, and she was grateful for it. Keeping busy was essential.

And, in so far as she was capable of any positive emotion, she knew she could be pleased with the home she'd bought, and its location. The East Devon seaside town of Teymouth, on the border with Dorset was familiar to her from childhood holidays there with her grandparents, and she liked its old-fashioned look and feel. The marine parade of Regency houses, looking as if they'd stepped out of a Jane Austen novel, overlooked a sandy beach, and the English Channel beyond, and, though she knew that now, in high season, the town was filled with holidaymakers, the small terraced house she'd bought was in a quiet, narrow road, set back from the parade, to the east of the main section of the town. Even so, it was only five minutes' walk down to the seafront, which also meant that the upper flat of the two into which the house had been divided when she'd bought the freehold was perfect to let out as holiday accommodation.

The owners had sold it with bookings already made, and Vanessa knew she would simply have to ensure the flat was clean and ready to receive visitors. The rent at high season was considerable, and because she had been able to buy the house outright she could use the rent as income, not for paying a mortgage. Although she would need to be prudent with her finances, she knew that, together with the modest but reassuring investments inherited from her grandparents, she could manage on her own.

For one fleeting moment a shadow darkened her eyes. Then, with a determined lift of her chin, she pushed aside the thought that had caused the shadow and started to tidy away the painting things.

By the time she'd cleared them away it was lunchtime, and she went into the kitchen to prepare a salad and a crusty French bread sandwich. It was simple fare, but nutritious and healthy, and all she needed. Fancy gourmet meals were a thing of the past now, and that was that. She poured some fresh orange juice and took her lunch through on a tray to the living room, where a small square dining table in the bow window caught the noonday sunshine. The house had no sea view, but all the houses in the street were painted in pale pastel colours, with tubs of flowers by the front doors and colourful window boxes. It was all very picture-postcard, for the tourist trade, but it made for a very pleasant environment to live in.

I'm lucky—so very lucky.

The words were a challenge, defiance, and a reminder. She *was* lucky—lucky to have had what she'd had, lucky in the wonderful memories of what, right up until the end, had been the most magical, miraculous time of her life.

I have to see the good things, only the good things.

If she became bitter about it it would only make the pain that tore at her, by day and by night, even worse. The heart-break was unbearable—it could never be anything else, she knew that with piercing agony—but the raw pain would fade. It would *have* to fade. That part of her life was over now, completely over. It could never come back.

But though she could say that with her mind, and know it for the truth, her heart was not so accepting. Like the pole of a magnet separated from its opposite, her heart kept drawing back to the cause of its agony, its complete and absolute fracture.

Markos—the man she had loved, adored. But who had not loved her back.

You can't force love—it wasn't his fault he didn't love me. Couldn't love me.

Yet, even as the exonerating words formed in her mind, another part of her let other thoughts slip through. Harsher words. Without exoneration.

He should have told you he was getting married. He should have had the guts—the decency—to do that, at least...

And back again came yet further thoughts, neither exonerating nor condemning, but resigned. Unflinchingly facing up to truths she didn't want to face up to, they marched their way into her consciousness, uninvited but unstoppable—just as Constantia Dimistris had marched into the apartment that fateful afternoon, at the most vulnerable moment of her life.

He didn't tell you for the same reason. He didn't love you. Because men like Markos Makarios do not fall in love with the women they keep as mistresses. Nor do they consider it necessary to inform them of their forthcoming marriages.

Because a mistress is not someone to love, someone to respect, someone who deserves consideration. She is there for sex, for admiration, for ornament, for possession, for pleasure.

Nothing else.

She shut her eyes as if to shut out the words, which were not angry or bitter, but simply truthful—however unpalatable the truth.

A mistress is all I was. All I ever was. I kept trying not to face up to it—

But she'd had to in the end. Just as now she had to face up to never seeing Markos again. There could be no other possibility.

It was over. Quite, quite over.

I have to face it, accept it and move on. Move on into the rest of my life.

It was essential. Because from now on, for the rest of her life, she had more than herself to think about. She had someone who was far more important than the man who had kept her as his naively adoring, expensively pampered mistress.

And far, far more important than herself.

She got to her feet, rubbing her back again as she did so. Clearing away her lunch things took only moments. Going back into the other room, she closed the windows she'd opened to expedite the drying of the freshly painted walls, then went into her own bedroom to put on a pair of outdoor shoes. As she put her worn house-slippers away inside the wardrobe she thought with painful wryness how shabby they had always looked amidst the racks of shoes and boots she had worn before. She was glad now she had kept the house-slippers though—they were something she had been able to take away with her, as the shoes and clothes that Markos had bought her had not.

She felt herself smile again, not painfully, but a smile that brought a softening to her eyes. High heels were a thing of the past in any case, and so were the flattering, beautiful clothes she'd worn for Markos. Now her sartorial needs were very different.

Comfortable, serviceable, practical—that was what she required.

Picking up her shoulder bag, she headed for the front door. Time for her daily constitutional—a brisk mile and back along the seafront. In the evening she would go swimming at the local public pool, doing steady lengths to keep her muscles toned and trim. Staying healthy was essential.

For a fleeting moment she remembered the luxuriously appointed private gym and the vast pool in the basement of Markos's apartment block. Then she put the memory aside. It was, like the rest of her time with him, irrelevant now.

Walking along the seafront in the warm sunshine, Vanessa gazed out over the sparkling sea. Her spirits could not fail to lift. People were strolling up and down, and on the beach children were playing. Her heart gave a little squeeze. Yes, this had been the right place to come to, a good choice. She could start her new life here, and as the years passed the pain would fade.

She lifted her chin. The pain had to fade. There was no alternative. The future was all she had now.

The past had gone completely. It would not come back, and nor would the person she had once been.

The mistress of Markos Makarios.

Markos eased the car out into the road, turning left as his satellite navigation had instructed him. The top was down—he'd lowered it as he'd come off the motorway some twenty miles back—and the breeze was ruffling his hair. Both he and the car, a sleek, throaty, high-performance latest model, were attracting attention from passers-by, but he did not return it. His entire concentration was focused on his goal.

And it was nearly achieved. Two more roads to go, so the sat-nav told him, and then he would have found her.

The pupils of his eyes pinpointed, his mouth tightening.

His anger, leashed tightly, was absolute, shimmering beneath the surface like a black roiling tide. As he inched the car forward in the solid queue that seemed to be occupying the seafront road he stared ahead, unseeing.

Then, from the corner of his eye, he saw it. His head whipped to one side.

Her hair.

That amazing tumbling mane, lifting in the breeze as she walked along the seafront, her gait brisk but steady. Familiar—but with a completely different balance to it.

He stopped the car where it was, right in the middle of the traffic, and vaulted out, striding between the cars parked along the seafront concourse.

She stopped dead.

Her face whitened like chalk. She swayed, and for a moment he thought she was going to pass out.

'Get in the car.' His voice was low, and vicious.

He saw her swallow, tense completely, face rigid, eyes seeing—yet unseeing.

'Get in,' he said again.

Around the car, other drivers were tooting their horns with irritation, calling out to him. He ignored them. Ignored everything except the woman standing there as if she were turned to stone.

Jaw tightening, he seized her arm and propelled her the way he had come. She was nerveless, unresisting.

He took her around the front of the car, opened the passenger door and thrust her inside. She collapsed into the seat.

Then, his face still as taut as a bow, he got back in the driver's seat and rammed the car into gear, jerking forward.

He did not look at her. Did not allow himself to do so. But he could see, as he changed gear again, that her hands were clenched in her lap, her knuckles white.

He drove in silence, interrupted only by the sat-nav voice giving directions, which he followed. They took him to the end of the seafront and turned him left, heading inland again for a short distance, then turning him right, then left. The road it took him to was narrow, lined with miniature versions of the houses along the seafront, lacking the iron railings and basements and pillared entrances, but neat and elegant. Hers was painted white, with flower boxes and two steps up to the front door.

He drew up outside the house, pulling the car alongside the kerb, which had 'Residents Only' restrictions marked along it. He ignored them, and cut the engine.

'Out,' he said.

She fumbled with the catch and he leant across, releasing it. She seemed to shrink away from him. He felt the anger roil.

She climbed out, pausing to hold the top of the door for a moment, then undid the flap of her shoulder bag and extracted her house keys. She opened the door of the house and went in, leaving it open.

He slammed his door shut, immobilised the car, and followed her.

Vanessa unlocked the inner door to her flat, the lower half of the house, and walked inside. Her legs were like jelly. She wanted to sink down on the nearest chair, but she knew she could not. Must not. Shock was still reeling through her, and she could feel a sense of sickness in her guts. Her heart-rate was plunging wildly.

This isn't good for me—this isn't good for the—

The sound of Markos slamming the front door made her jump, and then he was striding inside her flat, slamming that door too, so the room reverberated with the force. He was right inside now, his height crowding the room, his presence dominating it. She took a step backwards, feeling the edge of the table behind her, glad of its support.

Her eyes went to him.

Markos.

Emotion scythed through her, each stroke cutting her from her knees.

Oh, God, Markos—Markos.

Her eyes hung on him, each feature searing on to her brain. For an endless, reeling moment she was helpless to do anything but stand there, her brain trying to make sense of what her eyes were seeing.

Then, like a blow to her stomach, his words felled her.

'You little bitch! You two-timing, cheating bitch!'

For a moment she just went on staring, uncomprehending. His face was contorted, she could see, and fury was blazing in his eyes.

Her brow furrowed.

'What?'

Of all the things Markos might have said to her, what he had just hurled at her made absolutely no sense.

Yet her response seemed merely to infuriate him more. Fury seared in his eyes again.

'Don't give me that!' he snarled. 'I want to know one thing only—and, *Christos,* you had better tell me! Who is he? Just damn well tell me that—*who is he?*'

Incomprehension paralysed her. She could only stand there, hands clutching around the edge of the table, shock-waves jolting through her.

His face contorted.

'Don't try and blank me. Just tell me who it is! And don't

even *think* of trying to protect him because I swear to God I'll find out, and when I do—'

'*Who?*'

She could see his jaw clench, his entire body taut as a bow.

'What the hell do you mean, *who?*' he hurled back, his eyes like stabbing knives. 'The man you cheated on me with! The man who got you pregnant!'

CHAPTER NINE

THE WORLD SEEMED to stop. She could feel it grinding to a halt in the few fleeting seconds it took for his words to penetrate.

And, when they did, the shock she had felt up to then was as nothing, nothing at all. Disbelief, absolute and overwhelming, electrocuted her.

Blindly she felt for the back of the chair tucked under the table. Blindly she jerked it out, knowing with an overriding sense of protection for the child she carried that she must, *must* sit down before she fell down. She collapsed onto it, her heart hammering against her throat, hot and cold washing up and down through her body.

The world began to darken around the edges.

Instinctively she let her head sink down to her knees, forcing herself to try and take slow breaths. Equally instinctively her hand curved over her abdomen, sheltering the baby within.

'What—? Vanessa? *Vanessa!*'

There was fear in his voice, sudden, raw, completely negating the fury of a moment ago. He took two urgent strides towards her and crouched down beside her.

'Vanessa!'

She took a last, achingly slow breath, and lifted her head. The darkness receded, and there was just Markos instead. For one long, endless moment her eyes met his.

Then, swallowing deliberately, she said, 'I'm all right. I'm—all right.'

She straightened up. Abruptly, as if such closeness were too disturbing, Markos took a step back. His expression was a mix of emotions.

'Do you want me to call a doctor?'

His voice was short, as if he didn't want to make the offer but knew he had to.

She shook her head briefly.

'No, I'm all right,' she repeated The shock was ebbing from her, leaving behind something quite different. Something very calm, very still.

It's Markos, she told herself. Markos. Markos who has stormed down here and accused me of getting pregnant by another man.

She waited for the pain that the accusation, the assumption, must surely bring with it. Yet there was nothing. Only a great stillness inside her. As if something she had not realised still existed had just died.

But in its place came something else. A sure resolution that filled her, sustained her.

Slowly, she got to her feet. Markos started forward, but she held up a hand.

'I just need to get a glass of water,' she said, her voice quite calm. She glanced at him. 'Would you like a drink? Coffee? Juice?'

He gave a curt shake of his head. His face was still taut, his dark grey eyes stormy, yet wary too, and with something else in them that she did not want to see and did not study.

She walked into the kitchen and took a bottle of chilled mineral water out of the fridge, filling up a glass for herself. She took a few careful sips, then came back into the living room. She resumed her seat by the table and took another sip of water, before placing it carefully on a cork mat to avoid any rings on the surface of the wood. Her other hand hovered over her abdomen, as if shielding her baby from the man before her.

Then she looked up and across to him where he stood, tension and simmering anger and whatever else was streaming through him in every muscle of his body.

'What was the point of you coming here, Markos?' she asked.

His brows snapped together, as if both her question and the way she'd asked it had taken him aback.

'What was the *point?*' he echoed, his voice low and savage. 'You spend six months with me, then walk out on me without a word—a single damn word!—to another man, end up pregnant by him, and you ask me why I came here?'

She kept her eyes level on him. The same strange calmness was still inside her.

'That's what you think happened, is it?' she asked.

Anger darkened across his face.

'Don't take that tone with me—not after what you did! And don't even try and deny you're pregnant!' Accusation sliced from him.

Slowly, she shook her head. 'No, I won't try and deny it,' she said. What would be the point? The evidence was visible.

Something flashed deep in his eyes as she spoke. Then it was gone. She had no time to see what it was. But whatever it was didn't matter. Not any more.

'Then who was it? Answer me! Tell me who it was!'

There was a savagery in his voice that would have frightened her if she had not been so far beyond all feeling. She took in a breath, keeping it calm and even.

'So, tell me, have you any contenders for the man who lured me away from you? Perhaps the charming Cosmo Dimistris, tempting me with his expensive emeralds? He was keen enough, after all—he seemed to find the situation piquant.'

A hardness had entered her voice, but it seemed not to register with him. Instead, his own face tightened and a burst of Greek issued from him, sounding harsh for such a mellifluous language. Then he swapped to English.

'Do you think it *funny* to taunt me with your faithlessness?' His grey eyes were like molten steel.

Something seared in her face. Her chin lifted.

'Faithlessness? *You* are saying that to *me?* My God, you have a nerve!' Then, just as suddenly, her chin sank, her eyes closing momentarily. 'But of course you wouldn't think so. To you it was an irrelevance. I know that.'

Her face shuttered, as if protecting her from an unbearable truth, but a second later her eyes opened again. She looked at Markos—who had once been everything to her, who could now be only nothing.

The aggression seemed to go out of her, and it was with a supernaturally calm, level gaze resting on him that she spoke.

'Markos, I don't know what this is about, but there is no point you being here. Go home. Just go.'

Her voice sounded tired, very tired.

'I'll go—' he bit out each word '—when I have the truth from you—and not until then. Tell me his name. The name of the man who got you pregnant. Then I'll go.'

She looked at him, the man she had loved so devotedly, so besottedly. But whom she could not love any more.

'That you even have to ask is…is…' She stopped, defeated.

'But it must be someone! I have to know. I have to know who you went to—who you left me for. I have to *know!*'

There was a snarl in his voice and it made her flinch.

'This is absurd,' she said. 'Quite absurd. Insane.'

Then, as if a light had switched on inside her head, she understood. It was something inside him so primitive, so instinctive, that he could not see it in the rational light in which she—so agonisingly—could see it. For him, the logic was plain. He could get engaged to another woman, he could regard the woman who had shared his life for over half a year as nothing but a mistress to whom he owed nothing, not even honesty about his intention to marry, but *she,* the mistress kept in deliberate ignorance of her protector's intention of making another woman his wife, was expected to keep her favours for him alone, never stray to another man. She was expected to be faithful; for him the term did not exist. How should it? A mistress had no business knowing anything about a fiancée or a wife. He would expect—*demand*—that she keep to her appointed role as his mistress, reserving herself exclusively for his pleasure until such time as he chose to dispense with her services. And if she did not, he was entitled to feel betrayed by her, the woman he had honoured by choosing her for his bed.

Sickness filled her. Sickness and bile. But she knew it for the truth, for all that.

'Just tell me. For God's sake—tell me who it is!' His voice cut through her bitter reverie. 'If you are trying to protect him, then I give you my word—' he spoke through gritted teeth, in an extremity of emotion '—that I will not go after him.' He paused, chest heaving. 'I just have to know. You owe me that, at least.'

Vanessa's eyes rested on him dispassionately. Pitilessly.

'I don't owe you anything, Markos.' Her word fell like stones. 'Not a thing.'

'Not even the truth?' he snarled.

She felt her chin lift again. 'As much truth as you owed me. It's a two-way street, whatever you think to the contrary.'

His brows snapped together again, face darkening.

'What the hell do you mean? What two-way street?'

She took a heavy breath, laying her hand flat on the surface of the table.

'I'm not having this. I'm not dealing with your—your *medieval* attitudes.' Her lungs rasped. 'You may have thought of me as your mistress—well, I can't do anything about that. I can't change you, and I don't even want to. You think what you like, Markos. But I don't have to believe what you believe— and do you know? I don't. You can think of me as your mistress, but I never did and I never will. So I don't care if there are things you'll tell your mistress about and things you don't consider are any part of her business, because, after all, she's just your mistress. Just a convenient bed-warmer, someone to make you look good, someone to drape over your arm, a bejewelled, fashion-plate accessory! Just a rich man's toy. Not someone to tell anything *important* to! Oh, no, not that.'

'What the hell are you talking about?' There was incomprehension in his voice, and it might have made her laugh if she'd been in the mood for laughing. But she wasn't.

Her lips tightened.

'I'm talking about what was important to you, Markos! The little fact about you getting married!'

It was his turn for shock to immobilise him. She watched it happen, saw how the impact heightened his cheekbones, toughened the line of his jaw.

'*What?*' The word shot from him in total stupefaction. Then, as she watched, his eyes narrowed. 'Who told you that?' There was intense wariness in his voice; she could hear it.

For a moment she was silent. She did not want to remember that horrible episode in his apartment that last hideous day, when everything had come crashing down about her as if in an earthquake. But why should she shield him from what she had been put through so insultingly, so callously?

'It was your mother-in-law to be,' she said.

She saw the shockwave jolt through him. '*What?*'

'She wanted…' Vanessa's voice was steady, yet there was

a hollowness in her tone that made it hard to speak. 'She wanted to expedite the preparation for your forthcoming nuptials. She felt my continued presence in your life was...su-perfluous.'

Anger clenched through Markos's face.

'When the *hell* did Constantia Dimistris get hold of you?' It was not just a question, it was a demand.

Vanessa took a slow intake of breath. He knew instantly who had told her she was his future mother-in-law, and that tiny extra confirmation was like a weight crushing her down.

'The day I left,' she said.

Emotion contorted in his face again. He fought visibly for control. And failed. Greek burst from him then, and with a ragged breath he swapped to English.

'I don't believe this. I just do not believe it! On the strength of some uncorroborated statement from a complete stranger, you take it as gospel that I'm about to get *married?* God Almighty, how stupid can you be? Not to mention—' his face contorted again '—the little issue of trust! *Christos,* how could you? How could you just walk out on me because of what a stranger tells you, without even coming to me to ask if it's true?' A hand slashed through the air, sharp and violent. '*Thee mou,* how could you even *think* it was true? Haven't I made my views on marriage crystal-clear? I *will not* be pres-sured into marriage. I have no intention of marrying—ever.' His face hardened and his eyes bored into her like knives of steel. 'I told you to your face, that very day, that I would never marry.'

Vanessa's hand had tightened around her glass, nails whit-ening.

'Are you telling me you're *not* marrying Constantia Dimistris's daughter?'

It was difficult to get the words out. Each one seemed to grate in her throat like the edge of a razorblade.

'That,' he bit out savagely, 'is *exactly* what I'm telling you. And that you should have believed it for an instant makes me so angry I could—' He broke off, lips pressing together. 'How could you believe her?' he asked, his voice low and deadly.

There was a hollow inside her, like a chasm opening up.

'She was very convincing.'

'She lied.' His voice was flat, unarguable.

'Then why—?' She rested her eyes on him unblinkingly, while inside the chasm was swallowing her whole. 'Why did she give me twenty-five thousand pounds to "expedite my departure"? Why did she pay me off if what she'd told me wasn't true?'

'You took her money?' The anger flared again in Markos's voice.

Vanessa shut her eyes, then opened them again.

'I tore the cheque up and flushed it down the lavatory. Then I packed and left.'

'And it didn't occur to you to stick around long enough to ask *me* if what she'd told you wasn't a pack of lies?'

'How could it have been a pack of lies? She'd just parted with twenty-five thousand pounds. She wouldn't have done that if what she'd told me wasn't true.'

Both his hands flew up in a gesture of incomprehension and anger.

'It was to get you to go! And you fell for it like a complete patsy!'

'It was *twenty-five thousand pounds!*'

'So? Cheap at twice the price if it meant getting you out of my apartment to make way for the daughter I had no intention of marrying in the first place!'

Vanessa could only stare. 'But she couldn't possibly have handed over so much if what she told me wasn't true! Twenty-five thousand pounds is a fortune!'

Markos pressed his mouth together.

'Only to someone like you, Vanessa.'

She chilled. The way he had spoken sent slivers of ice down her spine. She looked around her for a second. The bright, cheerful, sunlit room, filled with furniture bought from catalogues and local homestores was a universe away from the kind of decor, the kind of apartment, that Markos Makarios— and his prospective brides and their families—were used to.

Markos was speaking again, dragging her attention back.

'And so, on the strength of a single uncorroborated claim, an attempt to bribe you so clumsy a child could see through it, you walked out on me. Without a word. Without an explanation. You took off, went to another man and got yourself pregnant.'

He glanced around. 'And to no purpose, I see. If this is your pay-off, you could have done a lot better for yourself. Were you counting on more, Vanessa? A wedding ring? Or, failing that, at least sufficient palimony and child maintenance to keep you in a villa in the south of France?'

She got to her feet.

'Please leave, Markos. I don't want you here. I don't want you anywhere near me.'

Her voice was dead.

He didn't budge. His eyes rested on her, cold as iron.

'Not till you tell me his name. Then I'll go. I won't break his neck, or beat him to a pulp. After all...' He gave a stark, hollow laugh, with no humour in it. 'You went to him willingly.'

She shook her head slowly, decisively.

'Just go.'

For one long, hideous moment she held his gaze. Then, with an abrupt turn of his heel, he strode to the door. She felt completely frozen.

He wrenched open the door. For a moment she thought he was just going to walk straight through. Then at the last moment he wheeled round.

The expression on his face shocked her.

'Oh, God, Vanessa—why did you do it? How could you have believed her? How could you have trusted me so little? We had so much together, and you threw it all away. All of it!'

Almost, she pitied him. Then, deep within her, she felt her child move and flex. Her hand clasped her abdomen, sheltering it.

'Please go,' she said.

And this time he did.

Markos reached out his hand and closed it like a vice around the bottle of whisky. But before he could refill his glass another hand grasped his wrist, pinioning him.

'Getting plastered won't help.'

Markos swore. It was in Greek, rich and inventive.

'Lay off me, Leo!' he finished.

His cousin prised his fingers off the bottle and removed it.

'Damn you to hell,' said Markos, and slumped back in his chair. 'And damn Vanessa, too. Especially her.' His eyes flicked to his cousin, sitting opposite him in the London apartment. 'How could she do it, Leo? How could she believe that manipulative harpy? How could she just walk out on me? Without a word! Without giving me a chance to explain what the hell Constantia Dimistris and my father were cooking up!' His face contorted. 'If she'd just *trusted* me, I'd have told her in a second it was just a lie. If she'd just trusted me enough to *ask*—'

'And what would have happened after you'd answered her, Markos?'

The voice that spoke was not his cousin's. It was female, sharp as a stiletto. His head swung in the direction of the voice.

'What's that supposed to mean?' he demanded.

Anna Makarios folded her arms across her chest.

'It's a simple enough question. Supposing Vanessa *had*

come running to you, and you'd explained that, no, as it happened you were *not* about to get married to Apollonia Whatever-her-name-is—what would have happened next?'

Markos stared at her. 'What do you mean, what would have happened? Everything would have been all right again. That's what would have happened.'

Anna pressed her lips together. '"Everything would have been all right again,"' she echoed. 'How very convenient for you. Vanessa would have kissed you besottedly, and gone on being devoted and adoring. The best mistress you'd ever had—wasn't that what you called her?'

'Anna...' Her husband's voice was placating. 'Look, I know you don't like the word, but—'

She didn't even look at him as she spoke. 'Shut up, Leo. This is important. It's not about a word, it's about an attitude. Your cousin had what to common-or-garden people like me and Vanessa was a *relationship*. For God's sake, they lived together for half a year—she shared his life! She wasn't his bloody *mistress*. At the very least she was his live-in lover, his partner, and calling her his mistress is a disgusting insult! Yes—' she cast a quelling look at Leo, who was trying to speak '—I'm well aware there are women who *are* mistresses, who leach off rich men to get a lifestyle they can't afford themselves, who trade sex for diamonds. But if you dare tell me that Vanessa was one of them I swear I'll clock you! She hasn't an avaricious bone in her body. She was just besotted with Markos, hopelessly in love with him—that's all!'

Viciously, Markos reached for the whisky bottle, which Leo had incautiously let go of, and refilled his glass. He knocked back a large mouthful and slammed the glass back on the coffee table.

'So besotted she walked out on me straight to another man!'

Two pairs of eyes turned on him incredulously.

'Excuse me?' Anna's voice was blank and Leo said something in Greek.

Markos's eyes were hard as steel. 'You heard me,' he said, his voice harsh, merciless.

'I heard you,' said Leo slowly, in English, 'but I don't believe you.'

'Make that two of us,' echoed Anna. 'There is just no *way* Vanessa would take up with someone else that fast. She'd have been crying into her broken dreams for months before anyone would have had a chance of mopping her up!'

Markos's chin lifted. His eyes flashed like swords.

'Oh, yes? Well, I'm afraid your touching faith in her attachment to me is misplaced, my dear Anna.' He gave a smile as savage as a wolf's and as bitter as gall. 'Or how come she's carrying another man's child?'

For a moment there was nothing but complete silence in the room. Then Anna spoke.

'Vanessa's pregnant?'

There was disbelief in her voice. Markos heard it, and his face hardened.

'Are you sure about that?' Leo echoed his wife's doubt.

Markos's eyes flashed, and he took another mouthful of whisky.

'Yes,' he said savagely. 'I am sure.'

'How do you know?' Anna demanded.

'I'm not blind. She's *pregnant.*'

'How did you find out?' Leo amended.

Markos turned to him. 'She did some modelling for a designer. Maternity wear. I saw the photos in an in-flight magazine. And when I finally tracked her down through the agency they'd used and confronted her, she didn't deny it. She even taunted me to guess who'd got her pregnant! Who it was she'd sought consolation with after she walked out on me!' The savagery in his voice was vehement.

'Did she tell you who?' Anna's sharp voice was jabbing at him in places he didn't want jabbed—places that were raw and bleeding inside him.

Markos's head swung towards her.

'She's protecting him. I said I'd break his neck, and though by the end I promised her I wouldn't touch him—' bitterness saturated his voice '—after all, she'd gone to him willingly— she still wouldn't tell me who it was. Not that it's done her any good. He's dumped her—paid her off with a box of a house in the back of nowhere, where she can't cause any trouble!'

Anna's folded arms clenched a moment. But her voice when she spoke was very controlled.

'Tell me something—how many months pregnant is she, Markos?'

'I don't know and I don't care,' he said tersely.

'Don't you?' she said. 'Although she's visibly pregnant? You know, I think you should care. I really think you should.'

His face darkened again. 'And what the hell do you mean by that?' he challenged.

Leo snarled in Greek, not liking the tone of his cousin's voice towards his wife. Markos's jaw tightened. But before he could say anything, Leo went on.

'Because you need to know, little cousin,' he said, very clearly, as if speaking to a child, 'for the following reason.'

Then he explained what that reason was.

Music pounded in his ears, heavy metal thudding through his bones, even though it was being torn away in the wind rushing over the open top of the car as it sped down the motorway, heading southwest. Markos let the noise saturate him, oblit- erating his thoughts. He didn't want to think, didn't want to feel. Didn't want to do anything except reach his target. And even that he didn't want to reach.

But every mile eaten up by the powerful engine brought him closer.

This journey, though physically the same as he had made that first time, at the beginning of the week, was totally different. Then, rage had fuelled him. Rage and outrage that the woman he'd devoted himself to had held him so cheap that she had gone straight into another man's arms—and got pregnant by him.

Now, a completely different emotion soaked through him. Far, far worse than outrage.

No! His mind cut out. He must not think—must not feel. Must not do anything, anything at all, except keep his foot hard down on the accelerator, giving the engine its head, riding it as if it were a surfboard in a hurricane.

The miles disappeared under the long, sleek bonnet. The junctions slipped by, one after another. Then it was the junction he needed. He slewed off the motorway, scarcely braking to move on to the road heading down to the coast.

He would be there soon, at a destination he did not want, but could not avoid.

It was déjà vu all over again.

The same neat terrace, the same sash windows, the same two steps to the front door, the same bright splash of flower boxes and doorstep tubs. He drew up in the space in front and cut the engine. Was she home? Walking along the seafront again? Having a check-up with her obstetrician?

No! He wasn't thinking about that—not yet. Not until he had found out the truth.

The truth he did not want. But which he knew he had to discover.

He got out of the car, shutting the door and immobilising the engine. Like an automaton he walked up to the front doo, rapped the knocker and waited.

After an indeterminate moment he lifted his hand to rap again, but even as he did so the door opened to him.

She stood there, staring at him. He saw the colour drain from her face. Saw the door start to close again.

He pushed forward, putting his foot over the threshold to stop her shutting him out.

'I have to talk to you.'

His voice was low, tense.

For a second she did not answer, then she spoke. Her voice was tight.

'You did enough talking the last time. I don't want to hear any more. I don't need to hear any more. Leave me alone.'

The sound of her voice scraped right over that raw, bleeding spot inside him, but he could not take any notice of that now.

'I have to talk to you,' he said again. 'I have to know—'

'No!' Her voice was sharp. 'No, you don't. You don't *have* to know anything—not a name, or an address, or anything. I don't care who you think I ran off with. I don't care *squat* what you—'

'It's not like that!'

His words cut across hers, urgent, imperative. His shoulders heaved.

'I have to talk to you. Vanessa—for God's sake. I have to know!'

He moved past her. He had to get inside. This was not a conversation he could have on the steps of her house. Carefully, as if she were made of red-hot metal, he stepped into the entrance hall. She lurched away from him as if he were equally red-hot, or contaminated with some deadly virus.

The movement away from him jabbed at something inside him. But he could not afford to feel it. Could not afford to do anything at all except get inside her flat and find out the truth, once and for all.

'One question. That's all I have to ask.' He said it as much to himself as to her.

Silently she let him walk into her flat, following him with her differently balanced gait. He turned to look at her, taking her in. Taking in the swell of her abdomen, its secret hidden within.

Something moved in him, so overpowering that it threatened to sweep away everything else. An urge so overwhelming that all he wanted to do was rush to her, wrap his arms around her. Hold her close, as close as he could, hold her and keep her and have her for ever…

'Well?'

Her voice was cold and distant. She stood looking at him, arms hanging loosely by her sides. She was not dressed in anything he recognised. And she looked, he registered, much as she had done the first time he had set eyes on her: with a natural beauty that took his breath away, unadorned by make-up or designer clothes or jewels.

Just Vanessa. Just herself.

And the child she carried…

Emotion knifed through him, but he would not let himself feel it. He was cauterised. He had to be.

He took a deep breath. Right down to the bottom of his lungs. It seared like a pyroclastic inhalation, scorching him.

'Is it mine?'

The words fell from him starkly, without volition. Brief and to the point.

She didn't move. Not a muscle, not a finger. Nothing.

'Is what yours?' she said.

His face flashed. How could she stonewall him at such a time?

'The baby,' he ground out. 'A simple yes or no will suffice.'

Her eyes were resting on him, but he could not read them. They were expressionless.

Something in them still hurt him, though.

Finally she spoke.

'The baby is mine, Markos. If that's what you came all this way to ask, you have your answer. Now, please go. I don't want to see you again. I don't want you turning up here again. It's over.'

'*Am I the father?*'

He saw her mouth press tight. 'I told you—the baby is mine. You're off the hook. Every man in the world is off the hook.'

'Don't be so bloody facetious!'

Anger flashed in her face. But even as she opened her mouth to bite back at him he rolled in, not letting her.

'No, Vanessa—don't do this! Look, I'm sorry. I'm sorry I made those accusations. I understand why you let me think it was another man's. You thought I was getting married to someone else. But I'm not. I made that clear enough the last time I was here! So there's no need to pretend any more. Just tell me if the baby is mine. That's all I need to know. Though why—'

He ran his hands through his hair. 'God, I don't understand any of this! I asked you outright if you were pregnant—and that was *before* that manipulative bitch Constantia Dimistris did her number on you! When I asked, you didn't have any idea in your head about my getting married—and still you told me categorically that you weren't pregnant. Were you lying? Or didn't you know? Or wasn't it even true at that stage?' He was thinking out loud. 'Because if you weren't pregnant then, it can't be mine—whatever Leo's damned wife says. But Anna insists that if you *look* pregnant now, then you must have been pregnant when you were with me—'

'Anna? Leo's *wife*? Anna Delane married Leo? Your *cousin* Leo? I don't believe it. She couldn't stand him!'

'Well, he obviously changed her mind for her,' said Markos impatiently. 'I'm not interested. There is only one thing I'm interested in, and that's if you are carrying my child.' His teeth gritted. 'So, are you or aren't you? Anna told me to ask you your due date.'

'Oh, did she?' Anger sharpened in her voice. 'Well, please inform her that my pregnancy is my business, and mine alone. And that includes my due date! Markos—go away. This has nothing whatsoever to do with you. I'll sign any papers you want. I'll certify to any child maintenance judge in the land that you are not the father of my baby. Will that damn well do? Get your lawyers, draw up whatever you want me to sign, and I'll sign it! But just get out of here and leave me alone!'

He just looked at her.

'I can't,' he said. 'Not if the child is mine.'

For one long, level moment she returned his gaze. Finally she said, 'Why not?'

It was said in such an offhand manner. As if it were a matter of supreme indifference to her.

His brows snapped together. '*Why not?* You can stand there and say. *Why not?*'

'Yes,' she answered, tight-lipped. 'I can. I've told you—this baby is *my* baby. No one else's. Mine.'

Disbelief swelled through him. Disbelief, frustration, incredulity.

'Don't be absurd! Every child has a father! And if the child you are carrying is mine, then I damn well want to know!'

'Why?'

Anger exploded through him at her obduracy. 'Because if the child is mine there is only one thing to be done!' He glared at her, fulminating. 'We'll get married.'

CHAPTER TEN

FOR A MOMENT there was silence. Complete and absolute. She could do and say nothing. Then, into the silence, Vanessa spoke.

'Married?' Her voice echoed blankly.

'Of course *married!* What else did you think would happen?'

'But you said you would never marry.'

He gave a heavy, exasperated sigh. 'Well, obviously I have no choice now, do I? If I've got you pregnant I'll marry you. End of story.'

Vanessa closed her eyes, then opened them again. Then, without a word, she walked into the kitchen and switched the kettle on to boil. Markos followed her, talking to her back.

'I'll need to have DNA tests done. I understand these days they can do them before birth. And as soon as paternity is confirmed we'll get married. How many weeks pregnant are you, and when is the baby due?'

Vanessa did not answer, busying herself with spooning instant coffee into two mugs and fetching milk from the fridge. The mundane physical activity helped to keep her calm. And it was very important that she stay calm. Very important.

'It's only instant, I'm afraid,' she said, as she poured hot water onto the granules, stirring the contents and topping hers with milk and his with cold water from the tap. Then she took her mug and sat down on the sofa by the little Victorian fireplace, its grate filled with a dried flower arrangement.

Markos had followed her out of the kitchen, ignoring the coffee she'd made him. She set hers down on the stone hearth and looked up at him.

'You can relax, Markos. I'm not going to marry you.' Her voice was very steady, her gaze level.

His eyes shot to hers.

'What the hell do you mean?'

'It's very simple. I am not going to marry you. You've made your views on marriage exceptionally clear—'

A hand slashed through the air. '*Christos,* that was before I knew about the baby!'

'How does that change anything? You spelled it out to me that last morning that I'd better not get pregnant—'

'But I was too late, wasn't I?' He turned on her. 'You were already pregnant, and either you didn't know or you deliberately lied to me when I asked you! Which was it?'

'I lied,' she answered calmly, not in the least troubled by the admission. 'I'd just discovered it myself and I was trying to come to terms with it. I was worried about how you would take the news. I found out pretty quickly,' she added bleakly.

'I thought I was just warning you off. I didn't realise it was already too late. How could you lie to me, Vanessa?' he demanded.

She raised her eyebrows. 'Very easily. You didn't exactly look overjoyed at the prospect of my being pregnant.'

'Well, why the hell should I have?' he retorted, glowering down at her.

'No, why should you?' she agreed placidly, as if what she was saying was so obvious that it didn't even need to be said. 'And you're not overjoyed now, are you? The last thing in the world you want is to marry me and be a father to my baby. So I'm not going to let you.'

'Don't be absurd!' he said shortly. 'I'm prepared to marry you, and that's that.'

She reached for her coffee and took a sip, replacing it carefully on the hearth.

'No, Markos, that isn't that. Do you really think I would marry you? Whatever for?'

'Financial security?' he jibed. His eyes narrowed suddenly. 'If the baby is mine, how do you come to be living here, in this house? Who's paying your bills?' The accusation and suspicion were back in his voice.

Vanessa's lips pressed together. There was a bite in her voice as she answered. 'For your information, I bought this house with the proceeds of the sale of my grandparents' house, which I inherited from them. They also had some investments. Not much by your standards, but quite enough for me to live on in comfort, together with the rental I'll get from the holiday flat upstairs, and maybe some modelling work now and then. I don't need any "financial security" from you or any other rich man—and therefore I have absolutely no need to marry you.'

Her calm precision seemed to infuriate him. She saw his eyes darken. With absolute self-control she kept her emotions tightly tied down. Losing it would only upset her—and her baby.

'This isn't about you, Vanessa! This is about *my child!* And, God help me, I won't have any child of mine born a bas—'

Her eyes flashed. 'Don't even *say* that word! You say it, Markos, and I'll hit you! There is absolutely no problem these days in being an unmarried mother, or in a child being illegitimate. But, my God, there'd be a hell of a lot of problems for a child with you for a father!'

'What do you mean by that?' he ground out. 'Any child of mine would have everything it wanted!'

Her eyes flashed with contempt.

It stung him. Stung him through the layers of anger

and the rest of the vicious, seething cocktail of emotions inside him.

'You mean money. That's all you can think about, isn't it, Markos? You and your precious money! Warning me off scheming to get you to marry me! Thinking I'd swan off to another rich man at the drop of a hat! Calling me your mistress like I was some kind of courtesan! Gritting your teeth while you arrogantly inform me that now I'm carrying your child you'll do me the supreme honour of marrying me and legitimising my baby—and making it crystal-clear that the very last thing you want to do is either! Well, thanks, but no thanks. I don't need that, and neither does my child. We'll do a lot better without you. So go, Markos. You're upsetting me, and I won't have that—not any more. Just go.'

His expression was unreadable, and she didn't waste any time trying to read it. Weariness and depression weighed down on her.

'I don't need you, Markos, and I don't want you. Neither does my baby. I never intended you to know about it. I don't know how you found out, but I wish you hadn't.'

Each word that fell from her was as heavy as lead. Yet when they were gone from her she felt no lightness. None at all.

'Then you shouldn't have modelled maternity wear, should you?' he said tightly.

She looked at him, seeing him but not seeing him. Refusing to let herself see him. Refusing to let her eyes drink him in the way they used to…

She must not let herself do that. That Vanessa was gone for ever.

'Is that how you tracked me down? I wouldn't have thought you'd have seen the photos. Not exactly your usual reading material, maternity magazines.'

'It was in an in-flight magazine. And—' His gaze

hardened. 'Can you imagine how I felt when I saw those photos? Or don't you care?'

'Why should I?' she returned, in that same dispassionate, tight voice. 'What possible reason would I have for thinking you'd take the slightest bit of notice—not after what you'd made so crystal-clear to me that last day?'

'I said those things to *stop* you getting pregnant! God, Vanessa, is that what this is about? Getting your own back on me because I said I would never marry you?' He inhaled sharply. 'Look, I can see why you were sore at me for saying that when that damn Dimistris woman fed you her garbage about me marrying Apollonia, but now you know that isn't true—was *never* true, just some ludicrous fantasy dreamed up by her and my father! So why are you still so angry?' He gazed down at her, brow furrowing. 'What's happened to you, Vanessa? I thought you'd be *glad* to marry me!'

The weight inside her was crushing her.

'Glad to marry you?' she echoed. Her lips pressed together. 'Don't you mean *grateful?* Because that's what a mistress should be when her protector offers marriage, respectability, his family name, lifelong financial security. She should be *grateful*. In fact—' there was an edge to her voice now, like the sharp facet of a jewel, diamond bright and very, very hard '—she should be *grateful* just to be your mistress, let alone anything more. And you know what, Markos? I *was* grateful. I couldn't believe you'd chosen me, *me,* out of all the beautiful women you could have picked! But you'd chosen me—and I was overjoyed, overwhelmed, overcome. *Grateful,*' she repeated, and it was as if the weight of the word might break her.

She looked at him, and her amber eyes were bright and hard.

'So grateful, Markos, that I did everything you wanted—rejoiced in the immense privilege of being the woman you wanted. And I never even imagined that all I was to you was a mistress!'

The jaggedness in her throat was scraping at her.

'*Thee mou,* you're obsessed by that word!'

Markos's face was drawn, as if his skin was too tight for the bones beneath, but as he spoke his tone was angry.

Fire flashed in Vanessa's eyes.

'No, *you're* obsessed by it! You hung that horrible label around my neck and strangled me with it! No! Don't even *try* and excuse it! Or yourself!' Anger was coursing through her now, released like a long-dammed tide. She should have let it out long ago, the moment he had first used the word. But she had been too much of a coward—too besotted, too devoted and adoring. She hadn't wanted to think Markos meant it, and then she hadn't wanted to face up to its impact on what she'd thought was between them—which had been so very different from what *he* had thought there was.

'To you I was just your mistress! A pampered bed-warmer that you took around so I'd be handy for whenever you wanted me!'

'That's not true!' he retorted hotly. 'I treated you with consideration, respect—'

'So much so you warned me off scheming to get you to marry me! You thought I might get pregnant to trap you! Well, I never asked you to marry me. I never asked for *anything.* Not the clothes or the jewels. I just wanted *you,* Markos. Only you.' There was a catch in her voice beneath the bitterness. 'Just to be with you.'

His cheekbones whitened, but she gave him no time to speak.

'I drifted along in some kind of fantastical dream, a fairy-tale come true. Doing whatever you wanted, abjectly grateful for the chance. Until you woke me from that dream—and it's as well I *did* wake up, Markos. Because otherwise I could have spent my life like that, being grateful to you.'

She rested her eyes on him. They were no longer hard or bright. They were very clear, and quite expressionless.

'But that's over now, Markos. It has to be. Because now the only person I must think about is my baby. I didn't intend to conceive it—from what the doctor has told me, the reason I got pregnant is because the antibiotics I took just after Christmas must have interfered with the Pill—but it's too late for regrets. Mine or yours. The only person in this entire situation who counts at all is the baby. And it's for the baby's sake that I won't marry you.'

'Why the hell not?' he bit out. There was incomprehension and frustration in his voice.

'Because it's not necessary. I don't *need* to marry you. I've dealt with the situation. I've walked out of an…an affair—if I can even call it that. I certainly can't call it a relationship, can I? Men don't have *relationships* with their mistresses. I've got my life sorted. I've got a good place to live, to bring up my child, with the seaside and clean air and good schools, and I've got enough money to do so. I'm making a new life for myself—a fresh start. I've joined a pre-natal mother-and-baby group, I'm meeting other people, making friends. I'm settling in and settling down. Me and my baby are going to be fine. I've got everything covered. Which means you're off the hook. You can go with a clear conscience. I'm not going to make any demands on you—none whatsoever—and I don't require any sacrifices from you, let alone marriage! I don't need you and neither does my baby.

'So go back to your gilded life and pick yourself another mistress from all the beautiful women queuing up for you. Make loads more money and spend it however you want, on whoever you want. Sleep with hordes of fantastic females. Have Taki and Stelios trail around after you, picking up your skis and handing you your jacket and paying your restaurant bills and smoothing your path so that nothing irritating ever happens to you, and be happy. Be happy, Markos. Because it's the life you want and the life you've got. And send down your team of highly paid lawyers with all their legally binding documents, and I'll sign anything you want me to.'

She ran breathlessly to the end and picked up her coffee, taking a large, reviving mouthful, needing the caffeine, fighting off the blackness that was drenching her. He was still standing there, hands on his hips, jacket pushed back, his face stark. A nerve was ticking in his cheek.

He looked as tense as a leashed tiger.

'You are carrying my child and I have responsibilities to it,' he said.

'I relieve you of all of them. Every one.'

'That is not in your gift. A child needs a father.' His voice was implacable.

Her eyes flashed, emotion biting through her. She knew she should suppress it, but she couldn't. Not any longer. Everything about his presence had been stretching her to breaking point, and now she snapped like wire pulled too tight. Her hands clenched around her coffee mug.

'A father like you?' Her voice stung. 'So our baby can grow up knowing that you never wanted him or her to be born, that you first checked that he or she was actually your child and then married me, the woman who'd been your walking, talking sex toy, out of duty, and that you think I trapped you into marriage by getting pregnant against your express instructions?' The words spat from her. 'Does my baby need a father like that, Markos? I don't think so. Some fathers aren't worth having!'

Her eyes bored into his. For one long, unbearable moment he just stood there as she hurled her judgement at him. His face was stark, as if carved with a knife. The colour had leached from his skin.

Then, without another word, he walked from the room. From the flat. From the house.

From her life.

Slowly, very slowly, she got to her feet. She felt immensely tired, as if weights had been tied to her arms, her legs. She almost stumbled as she carried the half-empty coffee mug back into the kitchen. Beside the kettle the other, untouched mug sat, cooling. Mechanically she poured them both down the sink, washing the mugs and placing them on the draining board. Then she looked out through the kitchen window, out over the tiny patio garden behind.

He's gone, she thought. This time he's gone. For good. He won't come back again.

She tried to feel glad. Knew she must feel glad. Knew that the only sane, rational response to what had happened had to be gladness.

Gratitude.

She was grateful that she'd been able to spell out for him at last what she knew she had been with him—to him. She'd purged it from her so that it was no longer part of her. Now she could move on, take hold of the rest of her life, which waited for her just as she waited for the child she carried to be born.

Her child didn't need a father who did not want them, had never wanted them. He'd never wanted her for anything more than a mistress.

And now she must only be grateful that he had gone, that she'd relieved him of all responsibility, all duty. His only reasons for wanting to marry her.

But as she stared unseeing over the summer sunlit patio she might have been staring out over an Arctic landscape as desolate as the icy bleakness in her heart.

What have I done? Dear God, what have I done?

The question tore at her like a polar wind, and the answer mocked her as savagely.

'Well?'

Leo's voice was expectant, requiring an answer. Markos gave it to him.

'The baby's mine.'

His cousin's expression did not change. 'And?'

Markos's jaw tightened. Leo was standing in front of his desk, towering over him. At least he was on his own this time, without the acid-tongued Anna, who was, so Leo had informed him, visiting her grandmother. Leo had just walked in unannounced by Markos's PA, who had bustled in apologetically behind him. Markos had dismissed her curtly. This was not an exchange he wanted to have. But Leo was not about to get out of his hair—not without answers.

So Markos gave him his answer.

'And nothing,' he said tersely.

Leo's face darkened. 'What the hell do you mean?' he demanded.

Anger flashed through Markos's eyes.

'Get lost, Leo. This has nothing to do with you!'

His cousin jabbed a finger towards him. 'Are you telling me that you aren't prepared to marry her?' There was scorn and incredulity in his voice in equal measures.

The flash of anger came again, and Markos's hands clenched over the wide leather arms of his chair.

'*She* won't marry *me*.'

'*What?*'

'You heard me.'

'I heard you, little cousin, but I don't believe you. Are you sure you actually used the word *marriage?* You're so damn allergic to the word maybe you couldn't even pronounce it!'

'I spelled it out in letters a mile high. She said no.'

Leo's expression was blank.

'Maybe the baby isn't yours after all, then,' he said slowly.

Markos's face hardened.

'That is not a possibility,' he said tightly. 'She was pregnant when she walked out on me.'

'That doesn't necessarily mean the baby is yours.' Leo's voice was dry.

Markos's eyes flashed. 'Are you saying she was unfaithful to me?' There was a belligerence is his voice that made Leo look at him hard. 'Vanessa was already pregnant when she left me—and she knew she was. But she lied to me when I asked her if she was pregnant.'

A frown furrowed Leo's brow. 'You asked her if she was pregnant? You mean you already thought she might be?'

The note of accusation was back in his voice again. Once more Markos's eyes flashed.

'I had no idea. None!'

'So how come you asked her then?' Leo pressed accusingly.

Markos shifted in his chair. He didn't want this conversation. He didn't want his damn cousin here standing in front of him interrogating him. And he certainly didn't want to answer any of his questions.

He threw his head back and glared at Leo.

'It was the last morning before she walked out on me. She started one of those damn conversations, you know the type— those "Where is our relationship going?" conversations...! And when that happens you know they're starting to cling, to make demands, to want more than they're going to get from you. When Vanessa started on me that morning it really got to me. She'd been absolutely no trouble up till then. Everything had been brilliant, the best ever. Damnit, I felt safe with her. She was exactly what I wanted, and I didn't want it going bad. I didn't want her spoiling everything. So I—'

He broke off. His cousin was standing there, looking tall, and tough.

'So you—' he prompted. There was still a hard look in his eyes.

Markos shrugged. 'So I spelled it out for her. I told her that

I was perfectly happy with her, that everything was great the way it was and that was that. She went all quiet—you know, the way women do when they don't like the message they've just received—and then she trotted out the "But what about if I got pregnant?" gambit. So I spelled that out for her, too.'

'Oh, you did, did you? Run it by me, will you, just for the record.'

Markos threw him a nasty look.

'Don't tell me you haven't done the same in your time, because I won't believe you. You know damn well how it goes. You tell them that you're not going to marry them under any circumstances, and if there's the slightest sign of them trying to get pregnant deliberately they are O-U-T.'

He was silent a moment, his gaze turning inward. A memory stung at him. The expression on Vanessa's face while he was spelling it out to her...

'It was bad timing,' he said abruptly, banishing the memory. 'Just bad timing.'

His gaze did not meet his cousin's.

'That's one way of putting it.' Leo's voice was dry.

The belligerent look was back in Markos's face.

'Look—I had no idea she was already pregnant. She'd just told me she wasn't. So why in God's name did she lie to me? It doesn't make *sense,* Leo. She must have known I'd stand by her.'

'Yeah, you've been a real tower of strength for her, haven't you?' said Leo.

Angrily, Markos jabbed his forefinger aggressively at his cousin.

'Don't give me that. I didn't know she was pregnant, I didn't know that she thought I was marrying Apollonia Dimistris—'

'From what you've said she didn't even know about Apollonia when you were doing your supportive spelling-it-out routine on her,' contested Leo scathingly.

His cousin stared back grittily. 'That was bad timing, too. That was the reason she walked out the same day—because that damn Constantia got to her before I had a chance to come back and make my peace with Vanessa.' Markos's face grew bitter. '*Theos*, if only I had stayed home that day, not gone into the office. But I had no idea—none—that Constantia Dimistris had turned up like a witch!'

'How come you didn't find out about that when you were looking for Vanessa?' Leo challenged. 'The concierge must have let her in—he'd have taken her name, so he should have told your security people she'd turned up that afternoon.'

An angry look darkened Markos's eyes. 'Vanessa wasn't the only object of Constantia's bribery. But with the concierge she found a more willing recipient. Since Vanessa told me what Constantia had done I had my people put the third degree on the entry hall staff—she'd handed out a massive bribe. Enough to shut mouths completely that she'd never been to the apartment. She didn't want me tracing back to her that she'd paid Vanessa to clear out.' He shut his eyes momentarily. 'I wish to God I'd known.' There was pain, as well as bitter anger in his voice. 'I still wouldn't have known where Vanessa had gone, but at least I would have had some kind of reason—I'd have got the truth from Constantia about what she'd done. I would have realised why Vanessa thought she had cause to hate me—'

'You mean, on top of her having cause to hate you because you rejected your baby—' Leo was merciless again.

Markos's head flew up. 'If I'd known Vanessa was already pregnant do you think I'd have said what I did to her that last morning? God Almighty, Leo, just how low do you think me?'

The look on his cousin's face as he threw his challenge at him was not merciful. Markos's response was defiantly belligerent.

'Look, all I knew was that Vanessa had walked out on me, without a word. She just left. I had no idea why—or where she'd gone. She disappeared off the face of the earth. I was sick with worry for her!' Breath dragged from him, and he went on, eye-balling his cousin. 'How the hell do you imagine I felt when I saw those photos of her in that in-flight magazine? Finding out she was pregnant because she was modelling maternity clothes?'

'Upon which, with unerring inaccuracy, you jumped to the wrong conclusion and stormed down to go ballistic on her,' finished his cousin. 'Great.'

Markos glared at him.

'I just knew she was pregnant, that's all. And of *course* I never thought it was mine—because I never dreamt that she'd lied to me in the first place! And why the hell didn't she put me straight, and admit it was mine? Especially after I told her that Constantia Dimistris had done a number on her!'

'I can't imagine,' said his cousin sarcastically. 'After all, you'd only accused her of walking straight out of your bed into another man's and getting herself pregnant by him. What woman could possibly take offence at that?'

'Damn it, do you think I *wanted* that to be true? Do you think I *wanted* Vanessa to be pregnant by another man? *Thee mou,* it *crucified* me, thinking of her with someone else, carrying his child…'

He broke off, his face contorting.

For a moment there was silence. Then, with the same narrowed look in his eye, Leo spoke.

'But this time, when you drove down again, you told her you'd been an offensive cretin to make such a foul accusation and it gutted you that she'd felt she'd had to leave you to bring your baby up on her own. You begged her to forgive you for being an insensitive swine, and you humbly asked would she please allow you to marry her and take care of her and the child you'd both created. That's what you said, right?'

Markos's jaw tightened.

'I said we'd get married. That there was no question otherwise now. And she turned me down flat.'

Something worked in Leo's face.

'Tell me, little cousin, does it ever occur to you that you are mentally deranged?' Markos's expression blackened, but Leo ignored it. Not giving him pause to retort, he went on. 'You know, any minute now I'm expecting to hear you told her that you'd be married once you'd got a positive DNA test on the baby—'

He broke off, and a Greek expletive issued from him.

'You *did,* didn't you? You told her that you wanted to check paternity before you married her!'

'Of course I damn well did! Do you think I wanted—?'

He fell silent. A bleak look entered his eyes. 'I just wish to God those tests had been around before I was born. It would have made life a lot—simpler.'

For the first time since he'd walked into his office his cousin lost the hard look in his eyes.

'What are you going to do, Markos?'

Markos's gaze slipped away, so that he was staring out into nothing.

'I can't force her to marry me. She wants to bring the baby up on her own. Obviously I'll create a trust fund for it, even if she doesn't want me to—and I'll make sure she's financially secure even though she says she's got enough to live on.'

'And what about the child? The courts would grant you access, at the very least. And you could always apply for custody.'

'No! God Almighty—do you think I'd do that?' Markos's eyes whipped back to Leo's.

Slowly, Leo shook his head.

'You might well not get custody,' he said. 'Vanessa's nothing like your mother. Not if she's going to live a quiet, respectable life as a seaside landlady. And you, Markos,' he added slowly, 'you are not your father.'

Dark slate eyes looked back at him, bleak as a winter's day.

'No?' he said, and his mouth twisted suddenly, hard and bitter and painful. 'Yet that was exactly the description Vanessa gave of me before she threw me out.'

It was night. Night and moonless and starless. Night high over the city, over the dark river flowing below. Night everywhere.

Markos stood motionless. He looked out into the night, hands closed over the high railing of his roof terrace.

Somewhere, hundreds of miles away to the south and west, Vanessa must be asleep, with her baby curled inside her.

So very far away.

His hand clenched more tightly over the cold steel edge. It felt like a cage all around him.

Inside him.

He let go abruptly and turned away, striding inside through the wide open terrace windows, stepping inside the long, luxurious lounge. Instinctively his eyes went to the sofa.

But Vanessa was not there.

She wasn't there, her eyes warm and glad, holding out her arms to him, waiting for him to come to her, for him to take her hand and kiss her soft, tender mouth.

She would never be there again.

Would never gaze up at him with her beautiful, adoring eyes. Never lie in his arms, her hair like a living flame across the pillows, never give herself to the ecstasy he could arouse in her. Never again.

I thought her my mistress but she was never that—never! She was always so much more…

A vice crushed his chest with physical pain.

She was always here. Always with me. Wherever I went, she came with me. She never left me…

But she had. And she would not be coming back. She would live her life, far away from him, not wanting anything to do with him...

The vice crushed again, so he could scarcely breathe.

She doesn't want me. Not for a husband or a father to her baby.

Again in his mind he replayed her harsh, condemning words, painting a portrait of himself that excoriated him.

Some fathers are not worth having...

And then, into the echo of her denunciation came another voice, his cousin's. Grim, harsh, but offering a single stark ray of hope.

You are not your father.

For a long, long moment he did not move. Then, with abrupt resolve, he strode into his bedroom. He walked to the closet and stared grimly around.

Somewhere, surely, there must be a suitcase.

CHAPTER ELEVEN

VANESSA SPREAD OUT the rug onto the sand and carefully lowered herself down on to it. Her movements were becoming increasingly ungainly, and the heat made her uncomfortable and restless these days. But after a fortnight of baking temperatures the weather had changed, bringing a refreshing breeze off the Atlantic and a shading haze over the summer sun. As she settled a cushion under her and reached into her beachbag for her book, she felt nothing more than pleasantly warm in her loose blouson top and wide, elasticated cotton cropped trousers.

She glanced down at the bump. It was far too large now even for modelling maternity wear. Advertisers always fought shy of showing women in the final stages when, no matter how well-designed, no maternity clothes could be flattering, only revealing. In any case, she'd be too tired to do any modelling now. At the time she'd been glad of the opportunity, even if it had come out of the blue via another of the girls who'd modelled the Levantsky collection.

A haunted look came into her eyes suddenly.

If I hadn't done that assignment Markos would never have found out about the baby.

Because she would never have told him. She knew that with a dull, drear certainty.

Opening the book, she did not immediately start reading, but looked out to sea instead, glad of her sunhat and the dark glasses taking the glare off her eyes. The tide was out and the beach was thronged with families and children enjoying the seaside.

She felt tired, but that was not surprising. The last stage of pregnancy would be like that, she knew, having assiduously read every pre-natal book she could find. She also knew it was important to keep as mobile as she could, so she made her twice daily constitutional up and down the seafront, and swam every other day as well, even though she was slowing down now. The water was comfortable, reducing the feeling of being so heavy. If the tide weren't so far out she would have gone in the sea now. Perhaps she would do so later, she thought, when it was closer in again.

She folded a hand over her swelling belly, as if to cradle her baby. It was strange to think of it upside down inside her, and she could distinctly see the outline of a foot every now and then. There was no activity now, though. That might be a sign, she had read, that she would get peaceful afternoons. Conversely, judging by the bouncing that regularly went on close to midnight, she wouldn't be able to look forward to early nights.

She let her thoughts run on quite deliberately, about the daily details of pre-natal life, and what was likely to happen once the birth was over. She was booked in to the local maternity hospital. Her bag was already packed, just as the books advised, and she had the numbers of three local taxi services, all of whom were willing to do either the scheduled run on her due date or an emergency one beforehand if necessary. Later, when winter came, she would buy a car. It was fine strolling around town in the summer, but in the winter it would be a different matter. Besides, local transport wasn't brilliant, and with a small child in tow having her own car was going to be essential in such a predominantly rural area. Some of the other mums she knew lived out of town, and if she wanted to keep in touch she'd need to be independently mobile.

She watched a group of children set up a game of beach cricket a little way away. Independence was going to be her watchword, she knew. Even with friends, and a supportive midwife and health visitor, she would have to rely on herself.

A pang went through her, but she put it aside. She could not afford to indulge in such things. She had remade her life and now she must live it.

You did the right thing. You know you did. There was nothing else to be done.

The familiar mantra formed in her mind.

Everything you said to him was true. You'll be perfectly all right on your own. You don't need him to sacrifice himself.

And it *would* have been a sacrifice, she reminded herself mercilessly. Everything Markos had said, during both those horrible descents on her, had made that pitilessly clear. And how could she ever forget what he'd said to her that last morning in his apartment, when he'd trampled on her frail, pathetic hopes so completely? For Markos, the worst thing in the world would be to get trapped into marriage by a pregnant mistress.

And that's what I did. It was my ignorance about the Pill that got me pregnant. That's the situation I'm in, and that's the situation I have to work out in the best way possible.

Her expression hardened.

And I don't need Markos to marry me out of an unwilling sense of responsibility to a baby he never wanted by a woman who never meant anything to him.

The pang came again, deep and agonising, as it always did when she made herself face up to the truth, sliding deep within her like a knife to the heart. It had hurt so much, facing up to the truth about Markos, but she had known it had to be done. For so long she'd lived in some kind of blind fantasy, adoring a man to whom she had never mattered. Then the veils had been ripped from her eyes and she had seen the truth of what she had become.

The pain of leaving him had been agonising, but it had been essential. For her self-respect, for her sanity; above all, for the child she carried.

Her face shadowed again. In her head she heard her own ruthless condemnation echoing harshly.

Some fathers are not worth having.

She would not wish that on any child—growing up with a father who had not wanted it to be born, had never regarded its mother as worth marrying, had even required proof that the baby she carried was genetically his.

No, a single-parent family might have its disadvantages, but it would never tear her child apart emotionally, never torment it with the knowledge of a father not wanting it, or its mother.

Her eyes strayed to the children playing cricket with their parents. Laughing and having fun, a family together. United and happy.

She looked away, back down to her book. A heaviness crushed her suddenly. If it was a boy, *she* would play beach cricket with him, she thought fiercely. He wouldn't need a father! He'd be fine without one—just fine! Loads of children grew up without fathers these days; it was perfectly normal.

After all, hadn't she grown up without either of her parents?

But you had your grandparents—they were your family.

She felt her heart tighten. She'd grown up without parents because of a tragic accident, not because someone had deliberately deprived her of them.

But I'm not depriving my child of a father! I'm keeping it safe from a father who would only cause grief!

And anyway, Markos had gone. Walked out without a

word. He wasn't coming back. She'd turned him down and he wouldn't offer again. He was probably off in some exotic location, staying in a fancy hotel or one of his half-dozen apartments round the world, with some gorgeous female to keep him company, to adore him...

The knife twisted again in her heart. She ignored it.

Markos was gone from her life. She was on her own. Her and her baby.

Markos wanted neither of them.

The sun was lowering to the west, but it was far from sinking yet. The beach was emptier, with many of the families wending their way back to their holiday accommodation for tea, but there were still a good few enjoying the last of the day. The tide had come in, and Vanessa had had her swim, wading into the water feeling more like a walrus than a woman. But she didn't care about how she looked. At this late stage of pregnancy she was fit and healthy, and that was all that mattered. Bobbing gently in the water like some kind of inflatable was very soothing.

She'd emerged, hair matted and salty, but not caring about that either. She'd let the warmth of the late afternoon dry her stretched maternity swimming costume, and then pulled her trousers up over it without even attempting to change on the beach. She would have a shower when she got back to the house, clean up properly then. Gathering her rug and her bag, she made her way slowly up the beach.

Gaining the promenade after an even slower ascent of the stone steps from the beach, she glanced at her watch. Her new holiday tenants were arriving this evening. The agency she let the flat through had told her they had said they would not be there before seven, so she had plenty of time. The upstairs flat had been cleaned thoroughly that morning, when the previous holidaymakers had left, and Vanessa had made the beds, set out a tea-tray, and put fresh flowers on the table and a couple of pints of fresh milk in the fridge, as she always did for new arrivals.

It was no problem having people upstairs. Most were families, and the sounds of children were merely a foretaste, she knew, of what her own life would bring shortly. This week, it was booked for a couple with an eight-year-old and a ten-year-old, travelling down from London that afternoon.

Back at the house, she put her sandy beach things in the kitchen sink and went to have her shower, sluicing and soaping off the salty water and lathering her hair into thick suds. Then she rinsed everything off and dried herself on a towel that seemed to be getting smaller every day.

She had just dressed herself in fresh clothes, a loose, cool cotton day-pyjama set in mint-green, and combed out her long tangled hair, when the doorbell rang. It wasn't seven yet, but perhaps the traffic had been lighter than expected. She padded heavily out of the bedroom, which overlooked the patio garden, and went to open the front door.

'Come in,' she said. 'You must have had a good run down from Lon—'

Her voice dried completely, and she felt her hand spasm on the doorframe where she stood.

Markos stood outside.

He was carrying a suitcase.

She could only stare. Every thought seemed to have drained from her. All except one.

It was the least relevant to anything but the immediate present, but it was the only thing that came to her.

'I've got people arriving at any moment,' she said blankly. 'For my holiday flat.'

'There's been a change of plan,' he answered. 'I'm the new tenant.'

'Excuse me?' Her voice sounded faint.

'You can phone the agency if you want. It's all been

arranged. The other family changed their minds. They've gone somewhere else on holiday.'

'What?' Vanessa was still stupefied.

'I offered them a five-star holiday in the Mediterranean if they'd agree to let me have their let for the fortnight.'

'You did *what?*'

'I offered them a five-star—'

'But *why?*'

She could feel herself leaning against the doorjamb. The space around her seemed to be coming and going. And everything in the entire universe was focussing on the man standing on her doorstep.

He was looking at her. There was something different about him, but she couldn't tell what. All she could tell was that there was a pain around her heart, a tearing, biting pain.

'Why?' she said again, faintly.

'I wanted to be near you,' he said.

His eyes were resting on her. They were dark, and grey, and they were looking at her from a place they had never looked at her from before. The pain got worse.

'This was the only way I could think to do it. The only way you couldn't throw me out again.'

Her eyes flashed.

'You don't seriously think I'm going to let you move in upstairs, do you?'

'I won't be a nuisance to you,' he said quietly. 'I'll look after myself—'

'Aren't Taki and Stelios going to do that, then?' she jibed.

'They're on holiday. I can survive without them. I know you don't think I can. But I can. I can survive without anyone, Vanessa. Anyone—except for one person. One person that I find, after all, that I cannot survive without. Not for a day, Vanessa. Not for a lifetime.'

His eyes were holding hers, streaming into hers. She felt

the faintness grow, drumming at her from very far away, but coming closer, louder. There were clouds rolling towards her, muffling everything.

She felt her fingers slipping from the doorjamb. The weight of her body was tipping forward, the drumming in her ears was drowning through her...

'Vanessa!'

He caught her as she slumped, taking her weight against him even though he staggered slightly as he did so. Tossing his suitcase inside the hallway, he propelled her inside, then with all his strength he lifted her and carried her into the living room, coming down onto the sofa with her still in his arms.

'Vanessa! Oh, God, Vanessa!'

He scooped her torso against him, Greek bursting from him in his agitation.

She came to with a low moan and tried to straighten, pushing back her tangled hair with one hand.

'Don't try and move! Just rest. Wait. Don't move.'

She didn't move. She just stayed where she was, her shoulders carried by his arms, her hip on his lap, her distended abdomen pressed against him. His body was warm, and hard, and so very, very familiar. It was his scent, his hands on her, his touch.

'Markos...'

Her voice was very faint, very tired.

'Markos.'

She turned her face into him and his arms tightened around her. The pain was tearing and biting, slaying her.

He was stroking her hair, soothing his hands along it and murmuring to her. She didn't know what he was saying, but the words flowed over her like a cool stream, like a warm balm, like arms drawing her to him, holding her, folding her. She lay there, being held by him, his hand on her hair, her face resting against the strong wall of his chest, inhaling the familiar scent, the touch and feel of him, his very being.

Markos. The man who was most dear to her. The man she had loved so much.

The man she still loved. Whom she would love for ever.

The truth of it blazed in her heart, unquenchable. She had never stopped loving him. *Could* never stop loving him.

Markos, who had come back for her. Come back to her...

She felt the tears start to slide from her silently, slipping one by one from her eyes, which could see nothing. She felt their moisture bead against her cheek, soak into the taut fine cotton of his shirt. And still he held her, and held her.

And now he was talking. She heard the words and understood them, low and resonant through the strong wall of his chest.

'Let me stay, Vanessa. It's all I ask. I won't trouble you or make demands on you. I just want to be near you, as close as you will let me be. Please don't turn me away. Please don't shut me out of your life. Please let me be near to you.'

The words flowed over her and into her, and as she heard them the heaviness of her body seemed to lighten. And more, far more than the heaviness of her body.

The tears slid from her eyes, faster now, until there was a stream soaking into his shirt, pouring down her cheeks, and she pressed her face closer to him.

The hands soothing her hair moved, cupping around her cheeks, feeling their wetness.

'Vanessa! Don't cry—don't cry!'

He held her face away from him, his own stricken.

She gazed up at him through blurred vision, her lashes wet, the tears flowing silently from her, and as she gazed the last of the heavy feeling turned to the sweetest lightness.

His thumbs smoothed the tears spilling from her eyes.

'Please don't cry. I didn't want to make you cry. I didn't want to upset you, or hurt you any more than I have already.

I've been so stupid, such a brute. You must hate me, and have every reason for hating me, but please don't cry. Just let me stay close to you and take care of you, our baby. Let me be a father to our child—even if you don't want to marry me or be my lover ever again, at least let me take care of you and our baby. I'll do anything. Anything I can. Anything you'll let me.'

She gazed up at him, her vision still blurred. And yet for the first time she seemed to see clearly.

'Do you mean that, Markos?' she said. Her voice was tremulous. 'Do you really mean that?'

'Oh, God, with all my heart, Vanessa. With all my heart.' His voice sounded as choked as hers.

He closed his eyes a moment, then opened them, searching deep into hers.

'Will you forgive me?' he asked, his voice low. 'Will you forgive me for being such a blind, stupid, arrogant fool? I treated you so badly. I took you for granted, took everything you gave me, and everything you said about what I'd done and what I am was true. I'm guilty of it all. I just didn't know. I didn't know until you walked out and left me just how much I needed you. And when I found out about the baby, thought you must have gone to another man, I was so twisted up inside I couldn't see straight. I couldn't see what anyone could have seen! And then, when Leo and Anna sent me back here again, I was even worse to you. I said such stupid, cretinous things to you. Can you ever forgive me? I was a fool, a complete fool, and if what I said then has made me lose you now, then I...then I...'

He came to a halt, his breath shuddering.

'Oh, Markos,' she breathed, her eyes softening, glowing like candles, illuminating the dark that had been all around him.

Slowly she reached up her mouth to kiss him. Slowly she felt her lips touch his, felt the long, low release that her touch brought him—and her.

Then she sank back into his arms, her head cradled against him. Peace filled her. He held her to him, bowing his head to brush his lips against her hair.

For a long, timeless moment he just sat there, holding her close to him, close to his heart.

Then, slowly, he started to speak again. The words came from very deep inside, from a place he had never wanted to look into again.

But now he did, taking the contents out of the darkness where they had lain so long and bringing them into the light, where they could finally shrivel and die.

'It was when you told me why you didn't want me to have anything to do with our child. That it would be better off without me for a father. A father who had never wanted his child to be born, who had never wanted to marry its mother, who hadn't even believed the child was his, who'd treated its mother as nothing more than a mistress…' He paused a moment, inhaling a heavy breath. 'Your words chilled me. To the bone.'

He was silent a while. She said nothing, giving him the time he needed.

'You see, you could have been describing my father. My mother—' his voice hardened unconsciously on the word '—my mother had been my father's mistress. She'd worked in a bar, at one of the Greek holiday resorts. My father picked her up, wanting nothing more than to amuse himself, the way he always did. She was ambitious; she wanted him to marry her. But to my father she was just a good-time girl, the kind who slept around with any Latin lover who took her promiscuous fancy. Not the kind of woman you married. The kind of woman you married was a respectable Greek girl, a virgin, protected and well-dowered, well-connected.

'When my mother told him she was pregnant he was furious. But he married her all the same. Because he felt that would be less dangerous to him than having an illegitimate child touted around by a woman who wouldn't hesitate to use the gutter press to bring him into disrepute. But the moment he'd married her, under duress, he mounted another woman as his mistress. He did it deliberately, to show my mother how much he resented having to marry her. It was my mother's turn to be furious. She stormed off to England to have me, and the moment I was born she started divorce proceedings. She wanted a fortune in alimony. My father contested it, demanding custody. It raged for years. Sometimes my father came to England, to see me, but always with my mother and her lawyer present. Because she was convinced that otherwise he'd whisk me back to Greece.

'They rowed all the time. I remember them rowing. My father hurling insults at her over my head, and my mother yelling back at him, telling him he'd never get me, not unless she got the settlement she wanted. My father demanded blood tests, asking how he could be sure I was his when she was such a slut. She called him a libertine, who'd been unfaithful from their wedding day. It went on all the time, one accusation after another, vicious and angry. I hated it. When I was young I didn't know what they were arguing about, but I knew I hated it. Hated it. When I was older I understood more of the words, more of the accusations. My mother tried to convince me it was all my father's fault, my father that it was all my mother's fault. It went on and on. Finally, when I was nine, my father's wealth won out. My mother had to make do with less money than she wanted, and I got taken away from her.'

For a moment he was silent again. Vanessa held very still. Then he continued.

'Even though my father had battled for me all my life, when he got me he sent me off to boarding school in Switzerland. He didn't actually want me—he just didn't want my mother to have me. He didn't want her to win. And when she'd lost the battle she didn't want me either. I wasn't any use to her after that. I don't think I was much use to my father, either. He still wondered whether I was actually his son or not. I think he felt that if I weren't, then keeping me away would make it less obvious to other people, because I wouldn't be around for comparison. I found it odd, because I knew I looked a lot like my cousin Leo. Then, as I grew older, I realised that that was another thing my father had been suspicious about—that maybe my mother had slept with Leo's father as well.

'When I was even older, and DNA testing had become viable, he had me tested. It showed that I was his genetic son, but it didn't make him any fonder of me. All it did was make him start going on at me to get married. He was feeling his age, feeling his mortality. He wanted to be sure of the Makarios dynasty continuing. Leo never showed any signs of marrying, not even after his father died, and that made my father even more obsessed about me getting married and having children—lots of little Makarios children—so he could be a dynast over them all. He wanted me to marry a good Greek girl, as he had never had the chance to do, thanks to my mother's machinations. He kept picking women out for me, trying to get me interested in them—like poor, wretched Apollonia Dimistris. It didn't matter that I told him I had no intention of marrying, let alone Apollonia, whom I scarcely knew except in passing. I kept mistresses, and I kept them in their place—the way he'd failed to do with his mistress, my mother. He didn't care what I said. He just went on and on at me every time he summoned me back to Greece—the way he did when we were at Leo's *schloss*. And that last choice of his was disastrous—Apollonia's mother is as bad as he is—totally ruthless about getting her daughter married off successfully. But of course—' his voice sounded hollow '—you know exactly how ruthless she is. Just as you know how ruthless I was prepared to be to make sure I never repeated my father's mistake when he was my age, with the mistress he ended up marrying.'

He fell silent again. Vanessa lay still, cradled against him. But his arms were very tight around her now. Too tight. Too tense.

And inside her was a heaviness that was far worse than the one she had known till now.

'Is your mother still alive?' she asked, lifting her head slightly.

She felt Markos tense again.

'No. She died when I was nineteen. It was an accident. She was at some party on a yacht in the South of France—the divorce settlement might not have been up to her expectations, but it was still a massive enough pay-off to allow her to be Tracey Makarios, socialite. She never remarried, you know; she liked the cachet of the Makarios name, and of course she could irritate the hell out of my father by dragging it through one scandal after another. She was found floating in the water, dead, in the early hours of the morning. She was drunk, and high, and naked. No one was very surprised. My father phoned me at university to tell me the news. He was elated. She was finally out of his hair.'

He fell silent again, and then Vanessa spoke.

'I'm glad she's dead. She's had the justice she deserved.' Her voice was quiet, but with something in it that had never been there before in all her life. 'And your father will have his own punishment now, and I'm glad for that too. Knowing that his son's mistress has repeated his own history.' She lifted her head to look at Markos. 'I never thought I'd be glad to have been your mistress, but I'm glad now. So very, very glad!' The fierceness in her face blazed from her eyes.

Reaching up with her hand, she slid it behind his neck and drew his mouth to hers, kissing it powerfully, possessively.

'They won't hurt you again, Markos. Neither of them.

Alive or dead. I won't allow it! They did so much damage to you, and I can't bear it!' Her expression changed. 'You said you would look after me, but *I'm* going to look after *you*. I'm going to take care of you and look after you and love you—but not blindly, adoringly, like some kind of infatuated teenage crush. This time I'm going to love you properly. Keep you safe from everything that has hurt you. And you're going to be the best father in the world. The very best. You'll never be like your ghastly father—never! You're strong and loving and brave and kind—'

'Kind? After the way I treated you?'

She brushed that aside.

'You were scared. Scared of history repeating itself. It was a knee-jerk reaction—not the real you.' She gazed up at him, lovelight in her eyes. 'This is the real you, Markos. Brave enough to come down a third time, after everything. Brave enough to regret what you'd done and make amends. Brave enough to walk away from what your shameful parents did to you and not let it poison you any more. Brave enough to take on a baby you didn't plan—and brave enough,' she added lovingly, 'to think you could manage without Taki and Stelios to wait on you hand and foot.'

He smiled ruefully. 'It was the prospect of doing my own laundry that really put the frighteners on me!'

She gave a soft laugh, and then, abruptly, her expression arrested.

'Vanessa, what is it?' Alarm was naked in his voice.

She half sat up.

'It's all right. It's just Bump moving. I was at an awkward angle.'

She levered herself up properly, resting back against the cushions of the sofa. Markos was staring at her in fascination and amazement.

'The baby moves?' he said, in a drawn voice.

'From side to side,' said Vanessa. 'Basically the head is downwards, and the feet are under my stomach. Look—there's one.'

She smoothed the material of her top taut. There was a discernible small extra bulge, protruding slightly.

'Thee mou,' said Markos faintly. Tentatively his hand reached out, hovering over the bulge, a look of stupefied wonder on his face. 'Can I—? May I? Would—will I hurt you—the baby?'

She smiled fondly. 'Of course you can, and of course you won't,' she said, and took his hand and lowered it to her, till it was pressed between her hand and his child.

'Hello, Bump,' said Markos softly, his voice strange.

For answer, his baby kicked hard. Vanessa winced, and said breathlessly, 'With a kick like that he has to be a boy—and a footballer as well, I think.'

'Do you know? Whether it's a girl or a boy?' Markos asked, his hand lifting away.

She shook her head. 'I didn't want to know. Would—would you prefer a boy?'

For answer, he leant across and kissed her softly.

'This one can be anything it wants,' he said. 'And, whichever it is, we'll get a second chance to get whatever it isn't with our next child.'

'Next child?' Her eyes were uncertain.

'Only is lonely,' he said. 'Leo was the closest I ever got to a brother. If you are willing, I would fill our house with children. And every one of them...' his eyes looked deep into hers '...every one would be blessed by the best mother in the world. As I—' he kissed her softly again '—would be blessed by the best wife in the world—if she will have me. Vanessa, you set me afire in the first moment I saw you, fighting off those pests in Paris. I wanted you then, and I went on wanting you, even when I was so arrogant and took you for granted;

even when I was so stupid and drove you away. I went on wanting you even when you'd left me and didn't want me near you or our baby. Even when you threw me out, I just went on wanting you. And it isn't just your beauty, even though it still sets me afire, and it isn't just my desire for you, though it consumes me. It's *you,* Vanessa, and your loving heart, *you* that I love so much I don't know what else to do except beg you to marry me, if you will. And if you won't, then please let me just be with you. As close as you will let me come.'

Her eyes filled with tears again.

'Oh, Markos—you're here already, in my heart. You'll always be there. Nothing can take you out. It hurt so much to leave you, but I knew I had to do it, that there could be no future. You didn't *want* to marry me, or to have a baby, and you didn't even think it was yours—'

'Don't. Oh, God, if I could unsay those words—'

'But even then I went on loving you, Markos. I knew I shouldn't. I had to tear you out of my heart. But I couldn't. I couldn't.'

He drew her to him, sliding his arm around her shoulders..

'I'm so glad you couldn't.' He rested her head against him, one hand holding hers in his lap. 'Will you marry me before Bump arrives?'

'We've only got a few weeks,' she said.

He dropped a kiss on her nose.

'I'll get Taki and Stelios on to it straight away. I'm sure they can get it sorted.'

'Or,' she retorted dryly, 'we could just organise it ourselves.'

He kissed her nose again. 'If you insist. It might even be fun, organising a wedding.'

'Just a little wedding,' said Vanessa. 'A very quiet one. With just the two of us.'

* * *

Carefully, Vanessa swung her legs out of the low-slung car and let Markos draw her to her feet.

'A taxi might have been easier,' she remarked.

Markos glanced ruefully at his low, long red monster, growling at the kerb.

'I'm making the most of this car,' he replied. 'Once Bump is out and about we'll need something bigger. Probably one of those SUVs, with its own trailer for all the nappies!'

He went back to the driver's seat to park the car, then came back to his bride, waiting for him by the entrance to the town's register office. A few passers-by glanced at her—she was difficult to miss now, especially in a cream silk tent—but Markos's car got most of the attention.

Until, that was, as Markos was about to lead his bride into the register office, the sound of rotors distracted them. They both looked up, and so did the people on the pavements.

The noise increased, and a brisk breeze started to blow that was not the prevailing sea wind.

'What—?'

Markos's words were drowned as something swarmed over the top of the building like a giant, angry wasp, sweeping over the roof and heading for the town park on to which the register office faced. At the same time a policeman on a motorcycle pulled up, dismounted, and strode into the park, gesturing with his arms for the central grassy patch to be cleared.

People duly scattered, everyone craning their necks to the buzzing, hovering helicopter.

At her side, Markos said something foreboding in Greek.

'What's happening?' asked Vanessa, a look of anxiety on her face. 'Is it the air ambulance?'

'Worse,' said her bridegroom grimly.

The helicopter descended onto the cleared area, with the infernal noise of the rotors finally decreasing, and from of the interior a tall, lithe man in a hand-made suit jumped down, then gave a hand to a woman in a brilliant scarlet couture outfit and a hat with a cascade of crimson feathers in it.

'Oh, my God, it's Anna,' said Vanessa faintly.

'And Leo,' added Markos.

'But this was going to be a very quiet wedding!'

'Not any more,' said Markos. 'We've been rumbled.'

With an air of resignation he watched Leo and Anna pause only to thank the policeman and bid farewell to the pilot, then charge across the road towards them. Greek burst from Leo, and he wrapped his arms around Markos in a huge bear hug. Anna came striding up to Vanessa and stopped dead in front of her.

'Don't you *dare* marry him if he hasn't *grovelled* to you yet!' she ordered. Then, without waiting for an answer, she lavished two huge air-kisses on each of Vanessa's cheeks. 'I can't kiss you properly because of this stupid lipstick,' she said, then stepped back, looking straight at her. 'He does love you, doesn't he? And he's said so, hasn't he?'

Vanessa nodded. 'Yes, he does, and he has, and he keeps on doing it. I can't seem to stop him.'

'Good!' said Anna fiercely, and turned on Markos. 'You just be *good* to her, all right?'

'All my life,' he said quietly. 'And beyond.'

'Good!' said Anna again, and then blinked rapidly. 'Oh, rats, I'm going to cry. And my make-up took *ages!'*

Silently, her husband handed her a large silk monogrammed handkerchief from his suit pocket.

'We're attracting the local paparazzi,' he announced laconically.

Around them a small crowd was gathering, and some were taking photos.

'That one in red is on the telly,' one woman remarked to another knowingly, if inaccurately. 'She's in one of the afternoon soaps.'

'Better get on with the wedding, love, or you'll be in the

maternity ward before he gets the ring on you!' called another
cheerfully to Vanessa.

'Smile, please—local press—*Teymouth Times,*' yet another
voice said, and a flash went off.

With a benign smile all round, Leo ushered his wife and
the bridal couple indoors.

'How the hell did you find out?' demanded Markos in
Greek, in an undertone.

'Don't be dense, little cousin,' returned Leo scornfully.
'Taki's sister's married to my pilot—you hadn't a hope in hell
of keeping it quiet. Just as well, anyway.'

He paused in the entrance hall and plunged his hand into
his inside jacket pocket, drawing out a jewellery case. He
turned to Vanessa.

'I'm cutting it a bit fine, I know, but this is for you. It's
compensation for having to marry my idiot of a cousin.'

He flicked open the case. Green fire flashed in the light.
Vanessa's breath caught.

'Oh, no, I couldn't—it's from the Levantsky collection!'

'I told Anna it would look perfect on you at your wedding.
And it will, too.' He lifted out the necklace, handed the case to
his wife, and moved to loop the emeralds around Vanessa's
neck.

'*I'll* drape my bride in jewels, thank you!' said Markos,
and took the necklace. 'And, what's more, I'll buy them for
her myself.'

Leo shrugged nonchalantly. 'I'll take a banker's draft from
you then. You can have them at cost, seeing as you're family.'

'Don't worry, you'll get the market price,' returned Markos.
'I can afford it. Profits on all my divisions are soaring.'

'Well, soaring profits on *my* divisions mean Anna and I are
going to give Vanessa the matching emerald bracelet for her
bride present—and I don't want any hassle from you, OK?'
riposted Leo.

'Could we just leave all your disgusting money out of this?' demanded Anna exasperatedly. 'And never mind about all these fancy green rocks. Just get on with the wedding. Vanessa shouldn't be on her feet so much.'

Carefully, Markos fastened the Levantsky emerald necklace around Vanessa's throat. Then he kissed her, very softly and tenderly.

'Ready?' he said.

She nodded, her eyes full. Happiness blazed through her. She couldn't speak.

'Then let's do it,' said Markos, taking her hand. 'Let's start the best marriage in the world.'

'Joint best,' said his cousin, reaching for Anna's hand. Together they followed Markos and Vanessa into the celebrant's chamber.

Outside, on the pavement, the photographer from the *Teymouth Times* waited patiently. His enquiry to the register office clerk to get the names of the couple, then a call to his newsdesk to run a search on 'Makarios', had struck gold. A stunning, tempestuous model, a dazzling red-headed bride one step away from the maternity ward, and not one but *two* handsome Greek multi-millionaires—not forgetting the top-of-the-range custom-built car gleaming at the kerb, and the helicopter parked on the green—yes, he definitely had the front page in the bag.

And all the glossy celebrity mags would be eating out of his hand for the photo rights...

He sighed happily, and checked his lens again.

Inside, oblivious to the photographer's forthcoming once-in-a-lifetime scoop, in a quiet, sun-filled room, with the scent of summer flowers from the bouquet on the table, two people made their vows. To love and to cherish each other all their lives, and to prepare the happiest of lives for themselves—and their child, waiting to be born.

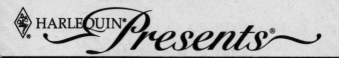

FOR *Love* OR MONEY

This is romance on the red carpet...

FOR LOVE OR MONEY is the ultimate reading experience for the reader who loves Modern/Presents, and who also has a taste for tales of wealth and celebrity and the accompanying gossip and scandal!

Jade Ferraro is a cosmetic surgeon, and Loukas Demakis is certain she's preying on the rich and famous to attract celebrity clients. He must seduce Jade to uncover the truth....

FOR REVENGE...OR PLEASURE
by Trish Morey
Available this June!

Available wherever Harlequin books are sold.

Coming Next Month

THE BEST HAS JUST GOTTEN BETTER!

#2541 HIS ROYAL LOVE-CHILD Lucy Monroe
Royal Brides

Danette Michaels knew that there would be no marriage, future or public acknowledgment as Principe Marcello Scorsolini's secret mistress. When she wanted more, the affair ended. Until a pregnancy test changed everything.

#2542 THE SHEIKH'S DISOBEDIENT BRIDE Jane Porter
Surrender to the Sheikh

He's a warrior who lives by the rules of the desert. When Sheikh Tair finds Tally has broken one of those sacred laws, he must act. Tally is kept like a slave girl, and her instinct is to flee, but as ruler, Tair must tame her. He knows he wants her—willing or not!

#2543 THE ITALIAN'S BLACKMAILED MISTRESS Jacqueline Baird
Bedded by Blackmail

For Max Quintano, blackmailing Sophie into becoming his mistress was simple: she'd do anything to protect her family from ruin—even give up her freedom to live in Max's Venetian palazzo. Now she's beholden to him, until she discovers exactly *why* he hates her so much.

#2544 WIFE AGAINST HER WILL Sara Craven
Wedlocked!

Darcy Langton is horrified when she finds herself engaged to arrogant, but sexy, businessman Joel Castille! But when Darcy makes a shocking discovery about her new husband, it's up to Joel to woo her back or risk losing his most valuable asset.

#2545 FOR REVENGE...OR PLEASURE? Trish Morey
For Love or Money

Jade Ferraro is a cosmetic surgeon, and Loukas Demakis is certain she's preying on the rich and famous of Beverly Hills to attract celebrity clients. He has no qualms about seducing information from Jade to uncover the truth.

#2546 HIS SECRETARY MISTRESS Chantelle Shaw
Mistress to a Millionaire

Jenna Deane is thrilled with her new job. Life hasn't been easy since her husband deserted her and their little daughter. But her new handsome boss expects Jenna to be available whenever he needs her. How can she tell him that she's a single mother?

HPCNM0506